THE GOAT PARVA
MURDERS

First Published in Great Britain 2014 by Mirador Publishing

First edition: 2014

ISBN: 978-1-910104-52-1

Mirador Publishing
Mirador
Wearne Lane
Langport
Somerset
TA10 9HB

The Goat Parva Murders

An Inspector Knowles Mystery

By

Julian Worker

Mirador Publishing
www.miradorpublishing.com

Chapter 1

The stalker trained his binoculars on the ground floor lounge window where Danica Baker-Clements could be seen in her underwear watching TV. Danica's blonde hair tumbled over artificially brown shoulders and the rhododendron branches twitched as the binoculars moved slowly over her complete loveliness. An owl screeched in the trees behind the stalker – the bird was catching mice in Doggett's Field near the Baker-Clements' house and had been disturbed. The warm night air was filled with the scent of honeysuckle.

The stalker was anticipating Mrs Baker-Clements removing her clothes during the evening as was the custom on Tuesdays and so intent was he on sharing every moment with her that he failed to hear the slight footfalls behind him. Danica Baker-Clements began to unhook her bra and the stalker's breathing increased in intensity.

As the bra fell aside the stone hit the stalker's skull rendering him unconscious instantly. He fell forward into the bush and then slumped to the ground, his glassy eyes surveying the lounge window but this time without binoculars. The assailant picked a bloom, placed it in the stalker's mouth, and clamped the mouth shut.

For Rosemary, thought the assailant, *the fight back begins.*

Two minutes later Tim Armstrong cycled down the Baker-Clements' drive and parked his bike out of sight behind the greenhouse. He was on time. He kept to the shadows created by the strong moonlight and soon knocked on the dining room window. Mrs Baker-Clements smiled, removed her last item of clothing, and headed to the window. They were seen only by a pair of lifeless eyes.

===========

The following morning Adelaide Hills was walking along the path between Doggett's Field and the river when her retriever, Bingo, started barking madly. He was always energetic on his morning walk but today he did seem particularly fascinated with some footprints in the mud. She pulled Bingo away and they carried on towards the Baker-Clements' mansion with Bingo looking back at all times.

"Come on, Bingo," she shouted, "any more of this prancing in the mud and I'll have to hose you down when we get home."

Bingo ran off into the bushes near the Baker-Clements' garden; a pheasant flew away towards the river. Mrs Hills then saw Carly Waferr heading towards her carrying the mushroom basket that accompanied her on morning walks during the week.

"Good morning, Carly, found a good crop this morning, have you?"

"I has," said Carly, putting an arm across the top of the basket, "and you can't have any. Unless you come for lunch of course," she added smilingly.

"Oh thank you, Carly, I'd love to, as long as they're not poisonous of course."

"Be no poisonous mushrooms in them woods," said Carly, "well not poisonous to me at least, but I'm probably immune now. I ate a couple this morn." She moved her head around in an anti-clockwise direction for five seconds before shaking her head vigourously.

"Are you sure – you seem dizzy?"

"That's just the hangover from the rhubarb and dandelion wine last night; Emma left for Edinburgh late so we shared a nightcap afore she went."

"What's she studying again?"

"Medicine – oh – look what your dog's found – a shoe."

"Bingo, you naughty dog, put that down immediately."

"How come dogs never find pairs of shoes; just one at a time? My shoes need throwing away, so I s'pose I should head to the animal shelter and borrow a couple of their retrievers and let 'em loose; hopefully they'd bring back a matching pair."

"This is a good shoe – Bingo where did you find this?" Mrs Hills gestured towards the bushes and Bingo flew off.

Carly Waferr was trying on the shoe when Bingo returned with the other matching shoe.

"My prayers have been answered, thank you lord," shouted Carly and grabbed the shoe from the retriever. "They fit, it's my day today," she added.

"Who leaves a pair of shoes for a dog to find?" wondered Mrs Hills as Bingo went back to the bushes.

"Ain't seen any campers," said Carly admiring the shoes, "and there's no tents around, 'cept those of Danica's admirers at her back door."

"Oh that awful woman and her loose morals - teasing the men with her low cut frocks."

Bingo came bounding up with a belt.

"Sorry, Bingo," said Carly, "I don't need a belt right now."

"Where's he finding all these things," said Adelaide, "is there a suitcase around?"

"Does you think…" said Carly, "that Danica's having sex outside with one of her friends and these are his clothes?"

"Alfresco fornication you mean?"

"Alf who," said Carly, "is he new in Goat Parva?"

Mrs Hills raised her eyebrows and followed Bingo into the bushes.

Carly was trying on the belt when she heard Mrs Hills scream.

Sounds like Danica and this Alf character have been discovered by our Adelaide, thought Carly, *I'd better hurry up, I don't want to miss anything.*

As she started towards where the scream had come from Mrs Hills came running towards her.

"He's dead," she shrieked, "Clem Shapiro's dead. I'm calling the police; he was bird-watching by the look of it," and she headed home following Bingo, who was carrying a glove that he didn't want to share with anyone.

Carly went to see the body.

"Got your just desserts, Clem," she said, "someone found

3

out about you and the birds you were watching." She looked through the rhododendrons and saw the Baker-Clements' house.

A peep show for perverts more like, she thought and headed back home to cook a mushroom omelette for her Wednesday morning breakfast.

============

Colin Knowles was eating his breakfast of black pudding, baked beans, and two fried eggs when his mobile phone rang on the kitchen counter. Knowles hauled his overweight frame to an upright position and having run his fingers through what remained of his brown hair, he answered the ringing summons.

"'Allo, Barnesy, what have you got for me?"

Rod Barnes, his assistant, replied in his normal clipped tones.

"Dead bird-watcher, sir, up by Doggett's Field. Lots of blood and the body has been interfered with after death by the looks of it."

"Charming, Barnesy, I was just having my breakfast as well – these people have no sense of timing, no respect for people's eating habits. I will be there when I have finished eating."

Knowles rang off and returned to the table but decided not to have more ketchup on his black pudding after all – why did people get bludgeoned to death so much - he couldn't eat breakfast any more without thinking of previous cases. He moved the black pudding to his cat's bowl – Gemma would love that after hunting in the garden and catching nothing as usual. Poor cat.

Knowles belched and lit a cigarette before remembering what his doctor had advised and put the noxious weed out by burying it with the others in the rubber plant by the door. Gemma came in through the cat flap looking upset and Knowles rubbed her head, before Gemma smelled the black pudding, rushed to her bowl and tucked into the food. *No murders for her to remember,* thought Knowles, *other than*

4

the mice of course. And that rabbit. He was brought out of his reverie by the phone – it was Barnes again.

"Bring some wellies, sir, it's muddy around here."

Knowles had them in his hand already; somehow Doggett's Field was always wet even in the height of summer. He got into his Land Rover and set off to Goat Parva, a place he'd always regarded as strange and immoral.

============

Knowles arrived at the crime scene and parked his vehicle by Barnes' white sports car.

What a show off, arriving at a suspicious death in a Morgan. Still, as he's only 26 he probably doesn't know any better, thought Knowles as he tried to put his feet into the Wellington boots.

His belly made life difficult especially in cramped situations like this and he vowed to start another diet tomorrow. "Lose some weight you fat sod," had been the considered opinion of the police doctor, for which Knowles had thanked him profusely and made a mental note not to cancel the next speeding ticket that the doctor received from the woodentops on the motorway.

Barnes arrived looking very fine in his Hugo Boss suit and tie.

"Name's Clem Shapiro, the butcher's assistant, aged 33, who seems to have been bird-watching, although I think the bird he was watching doesn't have feathers, in fact she doesn't seem to wear clothes that much from what I've heard."

"Bet you're referring to Danica Baker-Clements?"

"Heard of her, sir?"

"The surest thing between here and Leicester, Barnesy old son – not a prostitute exactly, but the same attitude without any money involved either. From what I've heard," added Knowles quickly before Barnes asked any awkward questions.

"Clem was hit on the head by a blunt instrument and suffered a severe head trauma that would have killed him

5

within a minute of the blow being struck – the medics will move the body as soon as you've looked at it – they believe he was killed around 11pm last night."

"What I don't understand is why he would have been watching her through binoculars from outside when everyone else just marches up to the front door and gets a closer look."

"Perhaps he was modest or thought he smelled strange, which might have upset her - he works at the butchers so perhaps he came here straight from work."

"He's a voyeur - a good old-fashioned, classic 'pervert' rather than a sexual athlete."

They arrived at the rhododendron bush and the medics nodded and smiled at the disheveled appearance of Knowles.

Knowles looked over the body and saw the massive bruise and matted blood on Shapiro's head – he was so glad he hadn't put ketchup on his black pudding this morning.

"Who found the body?" enquired Knowles.

"Bingo the retriever out on his morning walk."

"What on his own?"

"There was some human help, a Mrs Hills was accompanying Bingo at the time and she phoned us on behalf of Bingo."

"You see that's the difference between cats and dogs – a dog just goes and makes a fuss whereas a cat, a cat would have minded its business and carried on with whatever it was doing."

"Just as well we don't live in a cat's world then because the body would have stayed there for days."

"You said the body had been disturbed as well?"

"Yes, the shoes have been removed. He was found in bare feet, and he wouldn't have walked here without shoes – also his belt has gone and his jacket/coat/jumper too. It was cold last night and he would have been wearing something on his top half."

"So someone stripped the body of the nice items after he died? Is that a motive for murder or just an afterthought? There's no way of knowing who did the stripping of the body – we should ask Mrs Hills and her Bingo dog about that. I can't help noticing that his right hand's inside his trousers – poor sod, what a way to go."

"It's odd about the clothes because the binoculars are still here and they're worth more than all the clothes combined. Nikon they are, digital, the full Monty."

Knowles nodded to the medical team that they could take the body to the morgue.

"Right, Barnesy, our plan this morning is to visit Bingo and his owner and see what they have to say for themselves. Then we will come back here and visit Danica BC and see if she was aware of Clem here watching her."

"Why would she be aware of Clem watching her?"

"Because she complained to PC Davis a couple of years ago that she thought she was being watched, but he did a full investigation and never saw a thing."

"I wonder which way he was looking when he was investigating?"

"Or what he was looking at more like – she is quite beguiling and she knows it."

Chapter 2

Wednesday, lunch time

Knowles decided that he and Barnes should arrive at Mrs Hills' house in his Land Rover but that Mrs Danica Baker-Clements would be more impressed by Barnes' Morgan. They drove to Scoresby station, dropped off the Morgan and then chugged over to the Hills' house imaginatively called The Cottage.

After they knocked on the door of The Cottage there was a deep-throated "Woof, woof" from inside the house and a muffled shout from Mrs Hills, before she flung open the front door. Knowles and Barnes brandished their IDs. The smell of kippers filled their nostrils.

"Mrs Hills? I am DI Colin Knowles and this is Rod Barnes my sergeant – we'd like to talk about your grisly discovery this morning."

"Is that your police ID, it looked more like your library card, and it's expired – did you know that Inspector Knowles?"

"Ah, I was hoping you wouldn't notice – I left the police ID in my other trousers at home."

"You have another pair of trousers – I am so impressed, Inspector. Do come in and make yourself at home." Barnes suppressed a smirk as Knowles cleared a path to the sitting room where they were offered a seat on the couch. Knowles sat down and Barnes stood behind him.

"Should Bingo be present, Inspector?" enquired Mrs Hills. "He was the one who found the body after all."

"Bingo should be present yes, Mrs Hills – please bring him here."

"Bingo, here boy," shouted Mrs Hills. Bingo bounded into the room and started to eye Knowles' shoes surreptitiously.

"What kind of dog is this?" asked Rod Barnes, watching the creature from his vantage point behind the couch.

"He's a pure-bred retriever, Sergeant," said Mrs Hills patting Bingo and throwing an old slipper for him to 'retrieve' from the hallway.

"So, Mrs Hills…"

"Oh please call me Adelaide, Inspector."

"OK, Adelaide, can you let us know how you came to find the body?"

"It was Bingo that found the body of the Shapiro man – Bingo and I had walked along Sharrock Lane to the river and then around Doggett's Field when we met Carly."

"Who's she?"

"She lives just down the road; her daughter's just left to go to university in Edinburgh – she was telling me all about this after she appeared out of Hen's Wood."

"What did she say she'd been doing?"

"Collecting non-poisonous mushrooms, Inspector. She had a hangover too from her home-made wine." Mrs Hills flashed her pearly white teeth at the inspector.

"She particularly emphasised the fact that the mushrooms were non-poisonous?"

"She definitely mentioned it, yes."

"So at what point did Bingo here find the body then, Mrs Hills?"

Mrs Hills flushed a slight red colour. "He brought back a shoe."

"And then you went and found the body?"

"No, Carly and I continued to talk and she took the shoe away from Bingo and tried it on her foot."

"Right, so what happened next?"

"Well, Bingo is a retriever…" stammered Mrs Hills, "he went and fetched the other shoe."

"And then you went and found the body?"

"No, Carly and I continued to talk and she took the shoe away from Bingo and tried it on her other foot. She did remark it was unusual to find a matching pair of shoes."

Knowles shook his head in disbelief.

"Let me get this right, you were chattering with your Carly friend while your dog was stripping the body and interfering with a crime scene?"

"I didn't know he was doing that – it wasn't intentional. It wasn't a deliberate attempt to pervert the course of justice."

"Where are the shoes now?"

"Carly must still have them."

Barnes chimed in. "At what point did you suspect that there was something amiss?"

"When Bingo brought the belt for us."

"At what point did Bingo take off Clem's outer garments?"

"What? Bingo isn't that strong - he couldn't have done that – Clem was wearing a jacket when I saw the body."

"Did Carly come with you to see the body?"

"Yes, she did."

"Perhaps she took the jacket for some unknown reason?"

"I didn't see her do anything to the body although I did leave her behind with it when I went to call you, the police that is."

"We shall have to go and visit Carly. Just one final thing, Mrs Hills… Adelaide, did Bingo exhibit any other unusual behaviour during his walk?"

"He didn't really – he was distracted a few times but that's normal for him. If I think of anything I will let you know."

As they left Mrs Hills' home, Knowles sought Barnes' opinion.

Barnes stroked his slight goatee beard.

"She's not telling us the whole truth but I am not sure why as she didn't do anything suspicious."

"Too right," said Knowles, "she's fine, but that dog, it's weird, it was staring at my shoes all the time, and I wonder whether something else is missing apart from the shoes, belt, and jacket. Like a stool or chair or something. That dog couldn't have pulled shoes off a body, so they must have been untied beforehand, which suggests our Clem was in it for the duration and had either taken off his shoes or loosened them – but you wouldn't do that if you were standing up. He would also have loosened the belt if he was going to spank one out while watching Danica and his hand was in the appropriate place to do that when he was smacked on the head."

"Where to next, sir?"

"Carly's place – see if we can find those missing items."

"So you know Carly then?"

"I do, Sergeant, I just act stupid and ignorant for the benefit of our suspects."

"Do we charge her with receiving stolen property?"

"Unless she's sold them then no, but we'd have a real problem convincing the jury that Bingo was a thief and she was his fence. She's barking mad but that still doesn't put her on the same wavelength as Bingo."

"Where was Carly coming back from I wonder when Mrs Hills saw her?"

"I'd guess she was coming from Hen's Wood with a basket of hallucinogenic mushrooms."

Barnes and Knowles drove almost due south along the Leicester Road and parked in front of the postbox. As they got out a tall, artificially blonde young girl tottered towards them on high heels talking into her mobile phone. She pressed the remote control of her car and then jumped into the red Ferrari parked next to Knowles' Land Rover. She reversed into the road and roared off almost running the postman over in her haste.

A few seconds later a middle-aged lady in a bright blue cashmere cardigan came walking towards them.

"Was that Poppy Avon I heard accelerating away?"

"It was," said Knowles, "did you want her for something?"

"Who's Poppy Avon?" asked Barnes.

"She's Lord Avon's daughter and lives at Langstroth House," said the lady indicating towards the chimneys that were visible through the trees. "She paid for her chewing gum with a 50 pound note and didn't wait for her change because she was talking on her phone to her boyfriend and was so preoccupied that she forgot."

"Looks like a spoilt brat to me," said Knowles. "Anyway, it's Mrs Jargoy isn't it?"

"It is, Inspector Knowles, yes, how are you?"

"I'm fair to middling," said Knowles. "Have you seen Carly around, Carly Waferr?"

"She was in earlier complaining about her new shoes and bragging about finding poor Clem Shapiro's body near Danica's place."

"She's wearing new shoes – did you find out where she got them from?"

"From a charity shop probably knowing Carly – they looked like men's too with a few scratches on them."

"Any teeth marks?" Barnes tried to ask this question with a straight face, but failed miserably.

"I didn't look that closely…I am sorry I don't know your name?"

"DS Rod Barnes and I work for the boss here."

"Well DS Rod I don't normally look for teeth marks on any part of a person's anatomy or clothing – seeing someone's shoes from behind a counter is very difficult especially if you don't want them to notice."

"You noticed the scratches though."

"Yes, but they were deep and ran parallel down the side of the shoe – I noticed when Carly was leaving – I assumed she'd scratched them in the woods looking for fungi or whatever it was she was seeking."

"Thank you, Brenda – that's interesting information you have there."

"I should get back," said Mrs Jargoy, pointing behind herself, "I trust you'll be in soon for your nicotine patches, Inspector?"

"I will yes," said Knowles uncomfortably. "Anyway, I think I see Carly so we should be off."

"What nicotine patches," asked Barnes when they were out of earshot, "you smoke fags?"

"I used to wear them but they didn't match my skin tone, so I went back to the ciggies, but I have to try again to use those patches."

"Where did you see Carly?"

"I didn't - I just wanted to get away from that desperate woman."

"Desperate for what?"

"What do you think? Her husband gets his kicks from handling tools and doesn't even realise their daughter isn't his."

"Is that why she called Danica Baker-Clements by her first name? They're kindred spirits."

"Good spotting there, Barnesy – oh look who's in her garden – Carly Waferr."

They walked to the garden gate and called Carly, who waved to them to come in to her small vegetable garden. Bees were making for the hives in the western corner and the two men had to wave away an errant insect occasionally.

"Hello, Inspector Knowles – yes my bees are certainly making honey today – and who is this charming young man?"

"This is DS Rod Barnes."

"Hello, Mr Barnes, there's no need to be so deferential – you don't have to stare at my shoes you know, I have a face."

"Thank you, Miss Waferr." Barnes looked at Knowles and then glanced at the shoes again. Knowles nodded his approval.

"Talking of your shoes, Miss Waferr, I was wondering where you got them from – they're quite unusual."

Carly Waferr swallowed quite hard before saying, "I think I found them in the woods over by Doggett's Field. Why do you ask – have they been reported as missing?"

"The person whose shoes they were can't report them as missing because he's dead – I think you meant to say just now that you took them from a dog in Doggett's Field."

"Well a dog doesn't need shoes does it, so I thought I was a more deserving recipient of the windfall?"

"A windfall? These shoes didn't fall from a tree. They are an important part of a murder investigation; please remove them Miss Waferr."

Carly sat on a low wall and took off each shoe with great difficulty.

"They were cramping my feet anyway," she said handing them to Barnes, who looked closely for teeth marks and couldn't see any.

"And the belt, Carly, Bingo gave you that too," said Knowles.

"That damned woman spilled the beans – I will get even with her."

"Where's the jacket, Carly?"

"That Bingo dog didn't give me a jacket."

"Did you take it from the body when Mrs Hills went to report the murder?"

"No, I did not - Clem was still wearing it, I swear he was when I left him."

"Did you see anyone else around near the river when you were walking back?"

"I only saw Barry, Barry Janus, taking some pictures of the river near Hen's Wood. I waved to him. When I looked around a minute later he'd gone from my sight."

"Thank you, Miss Waferr," said Knowles and placed the shoes and belt in the plastic bag he had brought with him especially for the job.

"Now back to the station and change to your car so we can visit Danica Baker-Clements," said Knowles to Barnes as they left the garden. Behind them Carly Waferr was pulling carrots out of the ground with a great deal of anger.

============

When Knowles and Barnes arrived at Scoresby station Knowles left the shoes and belt in the lab for the forensic pathologist to examine. They transferred to Barnes' shiny sports car and headed back to Goat Parva on the Leicester Road. As they were about to turn into the Baker-Clements' drive Knowles saw a photographic tripod set up by the side of the road.

"Just pull into the drive Barnesy and stop – I want to see if that's anything to do with Barry Janus – I'd like to talk to him."

Barnes did as he was told and waited for Knowles to return. After a few minutes Tim Armstrong came pedalling up the drive looking rather pleased with himself. Barnes lowered the window and waved to the postman to stop.

14

"Are the Baker-Clements in?" he asked.

Tim Armstrong stopped smiling and got off his bike.

"I am not sure – I just deliver the post you know and don't wait around."

"We saw you earlier, about two hours ago, outside the post office and you were heading this way at that time. That girl Poppy Avon almost knocked you off your bike."

"Are you sure it was me?"

"How many postmen does this place have?"

"Might be an impersonator – there's so much fraud around these days, bogus this and bogus that, you can never be sure."

"I am sure it was you."

"Don't forget I don't just deliver in Goat Parva, I also go to Goat Magna, Melton Lonsdale, Frixton, and Madeley Waterless."

"Those last two are hamlets with about sixteen people living there. Goat Magna is smaller than Goat Parva now after the mine closed and Lonsdale is mainly second homes."

"That's all true but there are still deliveries to be made there. Anyway, I should be going I have a family planning event to go to."

Barnes nodded his consent and looked in the rear-view mirror to see Knowles heading his way.

"Well that was very interesting," said Knowles as he put his seatbelt on. "Barry Janus was there, taking pictures of a hedge, and he confirmed that he did see Carly Waferr this morning, but she didn't just wave to him – she made that cut-throat gesture and pointed to the rhododendron bushes where Clem Shapiro was lying. Janus went over there and saw Shapiro of course, but he swears Shapiro's jacket was missing – that he was wearing just a t-shirt and trousers. So either Mrs Hills is losing her mind and the jacket was never there or someone stole it after Carly Waferr's and before Barry Janus' viewings of the body. Doggett's Field is open so you'd think that either Janus or Waferr would have seen someone else, but the woods touch on the field between the Baker- Clements' property and Lord Avon's stately pile, so perhaps the thief could have hidden in the woods."

"Is that where Carly Waferr came from then?"

"Presumably. We should get the constables to see if they can find any evidence of someone waiting there for things to happen. I'll make the call when we get to the Baker-Clements."

"The other possibility is that someone was observing proceedings from the Baker-Clements' garden or from Avon's garden."

"Right, we should check that too. Did I see the postman just now?"

"Yes, we had a chat. I think he just scored with Danica and wanted to cover that up by claiming he was late because he'd ridden around the local hamlets delivering letters. He even claimed that the postman we saw earlier was an impostor."

"Of course it was - that's the only explanation isn't it? Not that he's a randy bastard who knows a sure thing when it's presented to him."

Barnes started the car and drove down to the front door. Knowles made the call for the constables at Scoresby to come over and search the woods where they joined Doggett's Field. Barnes looked around at the house and gave a hollow whistle. A pair of beautiful eyes watched him from the lounge and another pair of eyes were watching through binoculars from the garden.

============

Barry Janus was walking past the village shop when Tom Jargoy pulled up in his van.

"Hello, Barry, you look worried – what's the matter, have you run out of film?"

Janus leaned on his tripod and smiled.

"Just shows how much you know - I don't use film – I use the new digital technology."

"So what's up then?"

"That fat police inspector just spoke to me about inter-fering with Clem Shapiro's body – asked me if I'd removed his jacket. Why would I do that; he wasn't even my size?" Janus laughed, "plus I don't wear leather jackets do I?"

16

"How'd you know it was leather, Barry?"

"It's just a guess – he always had leather jackets did Clem – I suppose being a butcher he felt he had an affinity with the cow. Anyways, have they spoken to you – the police?"

"Why would they speak to me – I had nothing to do with it?"

"They'll be speaking to you I would have thought – just to establish where you were last night."

"I know they've been visiting Carly and bothering her – they took her shoes and belt. She was proper upset."

"You'd know all about visiting Carly wouldn't you Tom Jargoy?"

"You breathe a word of that to anyone and I will stick that tripod up your backside - you will know how the fairy feels on the top of the Christmas tree."

"Why so angry, Tom - your wife wouldn't mind – she'd just go over to Langstroth House as usual – but she'd wait for Lady Avon to go up to London first of course – normal behaviour for them all."

Tom Jargoy clenched his fists and felt the blood rising in his face – he glared at Janus, put the van into gear, and headed for the beer garden at the Badger & Ferret Inn. He'd get even with Barry Janus when he'd had a drink or two.

===========

Knowles looked at Barnes and wondered how he would react when he first saw Danica Baker-Clements. He'd probably stammer and play with the knot of his tie, which is what he normally did under pressure. Knowles didn't have long to find out.

She opened the door almost as though she was expecting them. She'd just had a shower and had her hair in a towel as she'd just washed it. The thin red bathing robe didn't hide her curves very well. Her face was still beautiful even without make-up. Barnes stared at her and then looked at Knowles, blew out his cheeks, and loosened the knot of his tie. Knowles looked at the floor and almost suppressed a grin.

"Gentlemen, am I double-booked? I don't remember either of you making arrangements to see me. Have you just come on the off-chance?"

"No, Mrs Baker-Clements, I am Inspector Knowles from Scoresby CID and this is my sergeant, Rod Barnes – we are here to ask you a few questions – do you have time?"

Danica glanced at the clock.

"I have a friend coming around 3pm, so we have plenty of time for questions and other things if we can fit them in."

She winked at Barnes who flushed bright red.

"Let's go into the lounge and get comfortable shall we?"

Knowles waited for Danica Baker-Clements to sit down before positioning himself opposite her. Barnes had sat down first and so was very close to the lady of the house.

"So Mrs Mrs Baker-Clem Clements," began Barnes.

Danica Baker-Clements leant forward and touched Barnes on the arm. "Danica, call me Danica, Sergeant Barnes."

"Danic Danica, is your husband in, is he around?"

"Roger, I have found that not to be an apt name by the way, hasn't been 'in' for about a month. He's an investment banker and is 'in' America setting up some new branches for the firm. I am here all alone, Sergeant, what should a girl do to occupy herself?"

Barnes stared open-mouthed and didn't answer the non-rhetorical question.

Knowles stepped in to continue the questions.

"Can we ask you what you were doing yesterday evening?"

"Indeed, Inspector Knowles. I had a friend over between 6 and 7 and another between 8 and 9. Then I watched TV until 10 when another friend came. I found it so hot in the TV lounge that I wasn't wearing much by the end of the evening – I think the thermostat is faulty, so it will be the same this evening."

She looked longingly at Barnes, who just stared back at her. He was smitten.

Knowles continued. "Were you aware that you were being watched, Danica, when you were in the TV lounge?"

"Of course, Inspector – it was Tuesday so there were

probably three people watching me when I was wearing very little in front of the TV. The number varies depending on the evening because of village meetings, whist drives, and committee meetings. I am essential viewing. It's all part of 'Village Life'."

"How do you know there were three people, Mrs Baker-Clements?"

"Binoculars do reflect light and I am sure that rhododendron bushes don't have reflective leaves. That creepy teenager Claude Avon looks at me through his telescope all the time from the house over there – I am amazed he can see but Poppy told me he can apparently. Someone was in the rhododendrons last night – it was either Barry J Anus – ooopps, did I mispronounce that - or that horrid butcher, Shapiro? Shapiro uses one of those golf seats and it leaves a distinctive hole in the ground; Janus has a tripod and takes snaps with his long lens, again leaving a distinctive pattern in the ground. You should check that, Inspector, while the ground is still soft. Carol Herald, that ugly woman who lives on Sharrock Lane and works at the animal shelter in Madeley, she sometimes sits in the woods and watches with her telescope. Roger saw her one night and asked what she was doing; she said she was looking for the Pole Star or some such lame excuse. She had a friend with her too, another woman who works at the shelter."

"Who was she?"

"I have no idea, Inspector. I wouldn't recognise her if I saw her again."

"Well, it was Shapiro in the rhodos, Danica, and someone smacked him over the head with a stone or an iron bar. Did you hear anything?"

"Not a thing. The TV was on and I was post…well happy anyway, so I heard no one being mugged."

"He was actually killed, Danica."

"That's sad for his family, but not for the animals he mistreated. Good riddance I say."

"Has anyone else watched you to your knowledge?"

"I think your PC Davis might have done; he investigated when I complained a couple of years ago that I was being watched, but he didn't find anything. He just sat on the couch with an erection, like you Sergeant, and stared at me. I think he might have crept around the garden looking for stalkers but ultimately didn't find anything. In the end I just got on with my life and didn't worry."

"You think he might have been out there?"

"I shouldn't wonder, but I don't take a roll call although I do receive a large number of Valentine's cards."

"Well I think we've asked you enough questions for one day, Danica," said Knowles. "We'll just take a look in the rhodo over there for any evidence of a golf seat."

"See you soon, Sergeant Barnes," said Danica, licking her lips in a provocative way as she closed the door behind them.

"Are you OK, Barnesy, you look shell-shocked."

"That's a real woman, whooo, those hips, I am aching."

"Tell you what," said Knowles, "I'll climb over this fence, but you…you can pole-vault over – look at you."

They hunted around in the rhododendrons and eventually found what they were looking for – a three-inch deep round hole made by a large man sitting on a golf seat.

"So that's something else that's missing – the jacket and now the seat. The murderer must have taken that seat at the time of the murder unless somebody else found the body before the dog and just thieved it."

"That's the sort of thing a cat would do, sir." Barnes knew that Knowles wouldn't ignore this.

"A cat-like personality yes – unless someone saw the murder and stole it after the murderer left. Anyway, this is getting too complicated. The last thing we should do today is go and see Clem Shapiro's place."

Knowles checked with the constables who were searching the woods to see if they'd found anything. There were a number of sandwich wrappers, a "Meat is Murder" sticker, and two beer bottles – nothing of any apparent significance, but Knowles left no stone unturned and asked for them all to be dusted for fingerprints.

Clem Shapiro's butchers shop was in Madeley Waterless but he lived in Goat Magna. Although it was about three miles by road, Goat Magna was only three quarters of a mile away from Goat Parva via the woods. Knowles believed Shapiro came through the woods to spy on Danica Baker-Clements as his vehicle had not been found.

As they were driving along, Knowles' phone rang.

"'Allo, Knowles, here – oh hello – really – a what – in his mouth – how long?"

There was a long period of silence and then Knowles rang off.

"This case just became slightly stranger, Barnesy old son. That was Dr Crabtree from the forensic lab. When they opened Shapiro's mouth they found a three-inch long stem from a flower, almost certainly a rhododendron flower, in his throat."

"There was no flower in his mouth when I arrived."

"Yes, I know, because that is something even you would have mentioned."

"What happened to the flower and why would the murderer have put a flower in Shapiro's mouth?"

"It's symbolic of something isn't it? What do butchers do with heads, the dead heads of animals – they sometimes place things in them such as apples – a pig's head with an apple in its mouth."

"Mimicking Shapiro and his decoration of dead meat?"

"The more troubling aspect of the case is this: Mrs Hills, Carly Waferr, and Barry Janus all saw the body and none of them mentioned a flower. We know that Shapiro's jacket disappeared from his body in the few minutes between Carly Waferr and Barry Janus viewing the body. We know that no-one saw the golf seat that Shapiro was using. There's two possibilities – either that bastard dog Bingo removed the flower from Shapiro's mouth or someone took the flower before Bingo started removing his shoes."

"So the person who took the seat took the flower too and then came back later for the jacket because Bingo disturbed them - they waited and then took the jacket after Carly Waferr left and before Barry Janus arrived?"

"Or the murderer took the seat and then someone else took the flower and a third person took the jacket."

"Don't forget Danica said she thought she was being

watched by three people one of whom we know was Shapiro; the second person might have taken the seat for more comfortable viewing and the third took the flower. Who would take the jacket?"

"Someone who lives close by and who might have seen something? Tomorrow we should pay a visit to Lord Avon and his family. You know what sickens me the most is that someone took a flower out of the mouth of a dead person with such force that the stem was torn off – that's what the lab said – the stem was torn."

============

Knowles and Barnes arrived at Clem Shapiro's semi-detached house situated at one end of a row of four town houses. The garden was overgrown and full of garden gnomes and dwarves. A magnificent buddleia covered half of the front door and as Knowles approached several Red Admiral butterflies fluttered away into the evening air. Barnes went around the back of the house to affect an entry using the keys found on Clem's body.

The back door was actually unlocked and Barnes opened the door gingerly; he'd once been bitten by a hungry dog whose owner hadn't been home for three days but Shapiro obviously lived alone – the dishes were piled high in the sink and the fridge door was slightly ajar.

Barnes let Knowles in at the front door and then scampered upstairs. Knowles looked at the pictures on the mantelpiece and then at some empty bottles in a corner.

"Sir," shouted Barnes from above, "you should come and see this."

Knowles trudged up the stairs and round to the right. Barnes was holding a few photos and smiling ruefully.

"Danica Baker-Clements in all her magnificence." He handed the pictures to Knowles who nodded appreciatively.

"Better than I imagined from today's encounter."

"No wonder the postman was smiling."

"I am surprised he could pedal his bike after two hours with…with her. Anyway, enough, enough of this lude

22

innuendo – we're only envious - have you see a camera that would have taken these pictures?"

"No – you'd need a long lens…"

"And a tripod. Wait till I see him."

"Sir, there's another couple of photos you should see." Barnes handed over the images and waited for a reaction.

"That's a strange picture – it's of someone else watching Danica BC I would guess and she's female – she looks familiar too. Sharrock Lane she lives on Sharrock Lane near the pub. Carol I think is her name. Oh, and what do we have here? Well, well PC Roger Davis in a wood somewhere with his binoculars and who's this young lady – I don't know her, unfortunately. We shall have to find out her name won't we, Barnesy?"

"We will, sir, but first I think we should have a beer or two and get some sleep."

"Sounds like a plan, Sergeant. It's your round isn't it?"

"It's always my round, sir, it's always my round."

Chapter 3

Thursday, 7am

PC Roger Davis was in a wood with his binoculars but there wasn't a young lady in sight. Instead, PC Davis was watching a young man, Todd Greggs, perform his early morning Tai Chi in Culpepper's Woods. Greggs loved the feeling of nature and being free amongst the horse chestnuts and oaks. He worked in London and had to leave Goat Parva at 7:30am in order to catch the train to King's Cross. Tai Chi was the perfect relaxing start to his otherwise hectic day at the stockbrokers.

PC Davis was fascinated by the precision of Greggs' performance and by his athletic prowess in maintaining the poses for the necessary time. The policeman wished he could do those exercises himself as he needed to relax more. As he was contemplating perhaps joining a gym he was distracted by Greggs bending over and touching his toes effortlessly. His assailant chose this moment to strike, knocking Davis unconscious as Greggs headed back to his house on Sharrock Lane for breakfast.

For Bruno, you cruel bastard, thought the assailant, as they placed some acorns in Davis' mouth, and clamped the mouth shut.

===========

Mrs Hills dragged Bingo out of the house and put him on a lead. Their normal walking route around Doggett's Field would still be blocked off by the police investigation so Mrs Hills thought they'd go through Culpepper's Woods for a change – they hadn't been through there in three months or more.

Once into the thick woods Mrs Hills let Bingo run free. Mrs Hills stopped for a rest against an ancient oak and saw

Claude Avon taking a picture of a tree silhouetted against the sky. He was using a tripod with a long lens.

"Hello, Claude," said Mrs Hills, "having fun?"

"Of course, Mrs Hills, I'm always having fun – the woods are quite thick here and I have to use a long lens to isolate just one tree's branches against the sky."

"My husband, Henry, was interested in photography before he died," said Mrs Hills with tears welling up in her eyes, "he loved landscapes especially in Africa and the Sahara Desert – which is where he was killed."

"I am sorry to hear that – how did it happen?"

"He was taking a picture of the sunset at the Merzouga Sand Sea and was concentrating on that so much he failed to notice that the camel had stopped and was going down on its haunches to let us off – he fell off head first and hit a stone."

"Oh look, Mrs Hills, your dog's got something in its mouth."

Mrs Hills looked and saw Bingo was carrying a felt hat.

"A walker has lost this in the woods, good dog for finding it." She took the hat and then looked at Claude, "this would suit you I think."

Claude tried on the hat as Bingo headed back into the woods.

"This feels really comfortable to me," he said, "I wonder if I should keep it?"

A look of sudden horror shot across Mrs Hills' face.

"I'd wait for a moment to see what else he brings back."

Bingo soon returned carrying a pair of binoculars.

"Take the hat off, Claude, and leave it on the ground – I suggest you go home now and pretend you've not been here today – Bingo, you naughty dog what have you found now – or more pertinently who?"

Before Bingo could run off, Mrs Hills put him on a lead and allowed him to show her where he'd found the hat and binoculars. Five minutes later she was making another phone call to the police from her home.

===========

Knowles was starting his latest diet and so breakfast comprised a black coffee and some toast with marmite spread on it. Gemma the cat looked disconsolately at Knowles; she had really appreciated the black pudding he gave her at breakfast as it supplemented her often meagre rations. If he kept up this non-meat diet she might have to actually catch her own food in the garden – needs must.

The instant Knowles bit into the marmite toastie the phone rang.

Knowles picked up the phone and pressed the talk button.

"Hello… hello are you there, Inspector?" Barnes waited for an answer.

"Mmmmm," said Knowles, "my breakie in my mmouth."

"Right, well here we go again, another body, this time in Culpepper's Woods – the same MO i.e. he has been smacked on the head by a blunt instrument. And I should tell you that it's Roger Davis…"

"Davis? Was he on duty do you know?"

"No, off duty, and I have to tell you that the body has been interfered with and the belongings have been scattered."

"Has that dog been involved again – that bloody Bingo?"

"It was Bingo that found the body."

"And who was Adelaide Hills jabbering to this time? It wasn't the Waferr woman again was it?"

"She says she wasn't talking to anyone else."

"That's rubbish – after yesterday's experience she should have known that the dog loves investigating crime scenes and messing them up – she was being distracted by either talking to someone or having a sly shag against a tree."

"Who'd have her, sir?"

"No, you're right; she was talking to someone - while her dog was removing items of clothing from the body. Again."

"Do you want to see the body, sir, or should I get the lab boys to remove it?"

"I'll be over in 20 minutes Barnesy to look at the scene – was he watching someone do you think? Is there anything in his mouth? Check that. See you there."

============

Knowles stooped over Davis' body and muttered, "Oh, Roger, what were you doing and who was it you were watching? Eh, Barnesy, do you think he's been moved or do you think he was here watching something or somebody?"

"This is a suitable depression in the ground to view someone or something over there in that glade especially if you have binoculars and/or a long lens."

They walked over to the glade. There were some individual footprints in the soft soil and they were slightly deeper than other prints where someone had been walking along.

"Someone was standing on one leg so all his/her weight was on one foot," said Knowles, "and she/he had quite petite feet with a distinctive tread pattern on the shoes – what could that be a heron impression contest? Look at me I am a flamingo."

"I'll ask forensics to take a cast of this footprint and then we can go around Goat Parva like Prince Charming looking for Cinderella."

"We can ask them whether they were aware that there was an unexpected guest at their ball."

One of the forensic officers waved them over to the body.

"We found these in the mouth, sir – acorns, seven acorns."

"That's disgusting – that probably means it was the same murderer as with Clem Shapiro," said Barnes. "I wonder if the number of acorns is significant, sir?"

"There are seven acorns – it might be a coincidence, but can you check to see if Davis ever worked in Sevenoaks?"

"I will, sir, when I get back to the office."

"Right, but before you do that let's pay our respects to Mrs Adelaide Hills and her bundle of joy, Bingo."

============

Mrs Hills opened the door and invited Knowles and

Barnes into her home. They walked through to the lounge and sat down while Mrs Hills leaned on the fireplace.

Knowles began, "So, Adelaide, what happened – what did your trusty beast retrieve this time?"

"A hat and a pair of binoculars – that's all this time."

"That's all – oh, so no shoes or belts then?"

"I checked the body this time and took an inventory and everything appeared to be there."

"Someone, or your dog of course, has rifled the victim's rucksack though and, we believe, taken the blanket the victim was laying on."

"How do you know that, Inspector?"

"It's because of the fibres on the victim's clothing at the front. Also, he had to be laying on something because there's no evidence of dirt or leaves on his clothes and yet you'd expect there to be some evidence of mother nature on his front if he'd been lying down in the woods, wouldn't you?"

"Bingo didn't bring back a blanket and I am almost 100% sure that the victim was laying on something when I saw him – I think it was a shower curtain rather than a blanket – it had those holes down one side where the rings go so you can hang it up."

"So the shower curtain was removed after you left and before Barnes here arrived?" mused Knowles.

"Was there anyone else around in the woods, Mrs Hills?" asked Barnes.

"There was nobody around."

"If that's the case why didn't you react when Bingo brought back the hat and go and investigate straightaway - given what happened yesterday?"

"I was being distracted by a partridge in the bushes."

"You've had the best part of an hour and that's the best you can do? Mrs Hills – with all due respect – that's utter rubbish – we found the hat in the woods nearby and there were two sets of prints in the soil and leaves, yours and someone else's. Now, who was it that you were talking to?"

"I don't want to get him into trouble."

"Who are you protecting?"

"Claude Avon – he owns an expensive camera and tripod

and he was taking pictures of the trees, but I know he uses that camera to spy on people especially his near neighbour, Danica Baker-Clements."

"Is there anyone who isn't spying on someone else?" wondered Barnes.

"Would Claude have seen you leave Culpepper's Woods, Mrs Hills?"

"I came out of the woods opposite Sharrock Lane so yes he could have hidden himself away and then gone back after I'd gone home to phone the police."

"Do you not have a mobile phone, Mrs Hills?"

"I do, but Bingo has hidden it along with some other items and I have no idea where – the naughty dog stole it when the battery was charging, so I can't even call the number and then listen for the phone ringing."

"How do you know it was Bingo that took the phone?"

"Because he takes items all the time, Sergeant – he buries things in the garden sometimes so I am expecting that my phone is under the azaleas or petunias. He places other items into containers; it's very strange behaviour for a dog."

"It's a real shame you don't have use of your phone because the crime scenes have been tampered with after you left both of them and before officers arrived. Someone is watching you leave the crime scene and then stealing something – a jacket, a shower curtain and I am not sure who or why? Whoever they are, I wish they'd make themselves known to us because they are probably holding on to some vital evidence."

"Does it have to be someone living in Goat Parva that's doing this?" queried Barnes.

"I don't think it has to be but it's more likely because of the time of day we're talking about 6:30 – 7am."

"You don't think someone's following Bingo and I do you, Inspector?" said Mrs Hills in a concerned manner.

"I can't rule it out but it's incredibly unlikely given that Bingo is such an inquisitive and alert dog – he'd notice straightaway. What I think happened today was that someone else was watching whatever Davis was watching and then came across Davis after the murder was committed."

"And stole his shower curtain?"

"Yes, unlikely as it sounds – perhaps it's better than whatever they have at the moment for their stalking activities in the woods."

"Anyway, Barnesy, we should be leaving and paying a few people a visit."

"Where will you be going for your morning walk tomorrow, Mrs Hills? Culpepper's Woods will be off limits to you as it's a crime scene," asked Barnes.

"I suppose we'll go up the river and head into Hen's Woods from that side rather than from Doggett's Field."

"Just one last question, Mrs Hills. Do you know of anyone who goes into Culpepper's Woods early in the morning to practice standing on one leg for longish periods of time?"

"I don't, but I have seen Mr Greggs, the stockbroker, coming out of there once or twice around 7am – he was carrying a bag I seem to remember."

"And he lives locally does he not?"

"Yes, I think it's 3 Sharrock Lane – but he works in the City of London so he's not around during the day."

"Thank you, Mrs Hills – we'll be seeing you – oh – where's Bingo? I haven't heard or seen him since we arrived."

"He's in his doghouse taking a break from being near me – I scolded him this morning for finding another body and he seems to have taken it to heart."

Barnes and Knowles bade their farewells and went back to Knowles' Land Rover.

"So, Sergeant Barnes, what do you make of all that?"

"How would a dog steal a mobile phone that was charging and so was plugged into the wall?"

"A very clever dog, Sergeant, not only to remove it from the wall, but also to hide the phone, charger, and cord so that the owner doesn't find it. I don't think Bingo would do that – I think someone took them while she was on her walk."

"A thief you mean or someone involved in the murders?"

"That's difficult to answer at the moment, but why would someone involved in the murders steal her mobile phone?

They'd have to know she was going to discover the body and then come back here to report it, so giving that someone more time at the crime scene."

"You don't think it's the murderer returning to the scene of the crime who's taking these items?"

"I don't think so – I think what we have here is someone who's going around knocking people on the head, but there almost seems a choice of people to kill each time. Danica BC said she thought she was being watched by three people and it seems like PC Davis wasn't the only person watching whoever it was practicing pirouetting in the woods. I don't think the murderer is killing stalkers – there's another motive but I have no idea what yet."

"So what's the plan, Inspector?"

"Well, Sergeant, I think I will drive us to Langstroth House to see young Claude Avon and then we visit Davis' home and see what we can find. Lastly we catch Mr Greggs after he returns from London."

"Sounds like a plan, sir."

"Oh good and while I am driving you can phone Constable Smythe and ask her to investigate whether PC Davis was ever stationed in Sevenoaks."

=============

Knowles hoped that his Land Rover would not look incongruous in the well ordered surroundings of Langstroth House. The lawns were mown into a chess board pattern and the topiary was immaculate. Even the sundial in the turning circle by the front door was polished to perfection.

Knowles tucked his shirt into his trousers and smoothed down his crumpled suit.

"How's the diet working, sir?" asked Barnes.

"I am just starting out so it's not had time to register with the fatty parts of my body."

Knowles pointed to the sundial.

"That's quite a sober decoration for the front of a house – normally it's either two nymphs copulating or three of them playing with a large stick."

"Why is it important to know the time before you enter the house?" wondered Barnes.

"It's more likely for when you leave – time passes slowly in houses such as this and it's necessary to check the time when you come out."

"So we're just interested in talking to Claude Avon?"

"Yes, but at least one of his parents will want to be with him."

Knowles pulled the rope that rang the bell in the servants' quarters.

After a minute the large wooden door lurched open and the butler stood there with a saturnine countenance – the result of a decade's practice.

"Gentlemen, how can I help you?"

"I am Detective Inspector Knowles and this is Detective Sergeant Barnes – we'd like to speak to Claude Avon if we may."

"Do you have an appointment?"

"Do we need one?" said Knowles sarcastically. "No! I don't think the police need to make appointments to see people who will be able to help them with their inquiries into a murder. Fetch him please."

"Please wait in the atrium here if you will." As he spoke the butler gestured to the area just inside the door.

The butler walked stiffly down the corridor and entered the door at the far end.

"A warm welcome as you'd expect from the upper classes," growled Knowles.

The room was full of the heads of various animals that had been shot on the family's estates in Scotland and transported down to Goat Parva to warn the locals about what would happen if they ever started to cause trouble.

The door at the far end of the corridor was flung open in anger and a short set man in tweeds marched towards them. About ten yards away from Barnes and Knowles he started shouting.

"What's the meaning of this – Claude, my son, involved in a murder? Preposterous, totally preposterous."

"Your son was in Culpepper's Woods this morning taking

pictures of the trees not far away from where a murder was committed. We can either talk to him here or we can take him down to the station for questioning. It's your choice."

"This is utter bunkum – I know the Chief Constable and I will phone him immediately about your intolerable accusations against my son."

"We are investigating a murder and we need your son's help in finding out what happened and when."

"Claude wouldn't hurt anyone and it's ridiculous to suggest otherwise."

"Lord Avon can we talk to him and find out what he knows?" Knowles was plumbing the depths of his diplomacy now and Barnes knew that there wasn't much left.

"Are you going to accuse him of murder, Inspector Knowles?"

"I am not going to do any such thing."

"Right, I have decided - you can question him in the presence of both myself and my wife and if I think there are any contentious issues then I will call my lawyer in London and he will be here in a flash."

In a flash car more like, thought Knowles as he said, "Of course, Lord Avon that will be exactly what the doctor ordered."

"Come through to the drawing room and I will go and round up the family," said Lord Avon.

Barnes and Knowles were escorted through to the drawing room and sat down on a long red sofa – the walls were covered with the books that wouldn't fit in the library and billiard room.

"How come people like this never have any Reader's Digest condensed books?" said Barnes looking at the musty volumes.

"Because they wish to appear learned and have a large amount of knowledge at their fingertips."

"I wonder how many of these books have actually been read by somebody."

"Barnesy, do you have your recording device with you?"
Barnes nodded.

"Quick - I hear footsteps, switch it on now."

Barnes put his hand in his pocket and switched on the device with the volume turned up high.

Lord Avon came into the room followed by a young man approximately 18 years of age and Lord Avon's wife, who was carrying a glass containing clear liquid..

"Inspector Knowles and Sergeant Barnes – this is my wife Antonia and my son Claude, whom I believe you wish to question regarding a murder in the woods this morning."

Claude looked nervous and sat forward with his elbows on his thighs – Antonia focused on the wall behind the officers as though thoroughly bored with the proceedings.

"Claude, I want to ask you what you were doing in Culpepper's Woods this morning around 7:30 and whether you saw anyone acting suspiciously."

Claude looked at the floor and bit his lip slightly before answering.

"Yah, I was there – I was photographing the trees against the sky using the long lens and tripod – the only people I definitely saw were the Hills woman and her dog Bongo or whatever it's called and also Greggs the stockbroker man, doing his Tai Chi in a clearing in the woods."

"Does this Tie Chee involve standing on one leg for a while?"

"It can do – it depends on what routines you choose."

"So that explains the single footprints that we found in the leafy glade – there was more downward pressure on those footprints than the others."

Barnes interjected. "You said people I definitely saw – who else did you think you might have seen?"

At this point Antonia Avon suddenly yawned. She got up and walked out of the room draining the remaining contents of her glass.

"Who was it you might have seen, Claude?"

"Well I thought I saw that Barry Janus man over by the badger sett but I couldn't be sure as there were many branches in the way; I am pretty sure I saw Carol Herald running away from the glade in the direction of Madeley Waterless, but again I can't be sure. There was someone else too near the glade, but they were lying down – I just saw the light reflect off their binoculars once or twice. Poppy was there too practicing her Buddhism."

"There was quite a crowd out this morning wasn't there?"

"No more so than usual," said Claude. "Whenever I am taking pictures over there I am never alone. The only person I saw this morning who's not normally there was Mrs Hills."

"And she was only there because her usual morning walk around Doggett's Field was blocked off because of the previous murder."

"Yah, right – of course – that was yesterday morning – seems ages ago now; I saw Carol Herald then too – she was lurking in the woods by the Baker-Clements house."

"Are you sure it was her?"

"Almost 100% sure; I got a better look than today as she was staying still hoping not to be seen I think."

Antonia Avon came tottering back into the room and sat down in a high-backed chair.

Lord Avon glared at her and her full glass.

"What's the matter, darling – just having a drink to help me through the day. Now what's Claude been telling you, Inspector?"

"He was telling me about seeing Carol Herald yesterday morning in the woods near here."

"Oh yes her – is that her name – Herald? She's always hanging around the woods watching people going about their business. I have felt her watching me when I go through the woods. She's not the worst though – I am sure that Janus man takes pictures of people which is a huge invasion of privacy."

"Why didn't you mention this to me, Antonia?"

"Why would I mention it, Henry, it's of no interest to you, darling because you never go into the woods and do anything that people would want to watch do you?"

Lord Avon flushed red and Knowles wasn't sure whether he was angry or embarrassed. What was Lady Avon hinting at?

Lord Avon had had enough of proceedings and said so.

"I think we've seen and heard enough for now, thank you everyone," said Knowles and stood up, a move that prompted Barnes to stand up too.

"What time is it, Sergeant?" asked Knowles.

"It's 1:30 pm on September 24th," replied Barnes as nonchalantly as he could.

"September the 24th, what a good day that is," said Knowles, "autumn is just beginning."

They were escorted off the premises by the butler, whose name they never did learn. When they reached the sanctuary and familiarity of Knowles' Land Rover they both breathed a sigh of relief and anxiously replayed the recording, which came across loud and clear.

"What was Antonia Avon drinking do you think?" grinned Knowles.

"A truth serum and her candour really got up her husband's nose."

"I wonder why she goes walking in the woods – she'd bump into the trees. She almost missed that chair you know when she came in the second time."

"Yes, I saw the look of relief on her face when her backside hit the seat and not the floor."

"More importantly why does her husband go into the woods and what does he do there that he wants to keep hidden from public knowledge?"

"I bet Carol Herald knows as she seems to be where all the action is."

Knowles thought about Barnes' statement.

"Right – good point – when we've been to Davis' home we should split – you go and see Carol and I will visit Mr Greggs."

"That sounds like a great idea because they both live on Sharrock Lane and we could go to the Badger afterwards for a pint and compare notes."

"It's a date, Barnesy. Right, which way to Madeley Waterless from here?"

"South along Leicester Road and then first left after the traffic lights. That was something I didn't understand about Claude's statement – he said that Carol Herald was running

36

towards Madeley Waterless – why would she be running away from her home rather than towards it?"

"She works at the animal shelter there I believe, so perhaps she was heading towards her place of work – perhaps she runs to work? It might well rule her out of our considerations for the person who interferes with the crime scenes after Mrs Hills has seen the bodies. Turning up with a shower curtain at work is quite a unique thing to do, so we should ask them when we go there, perhaps tomorrow."

"All of a sudden we have a lot of leads and questions and fewer and fewer answers."

============

Madeley Waterless was a tiny place of one street and Davis' home was the first house on the right as they came through the village from Goat Parva. The forensic team had already paid a visit so the village constable was able to let Knowles and Barnes in to the property.

"Right, let's see what the boys in white have left for us," said Knowles, "and just for a change I'll go upstairs – I need the exercise as part of my new dietary regime."

Barnes looked around the downstairs, but got the impression quite quickly that something was missing, that Davis had almost expected this situation to happen and had covered his tracks accordingly. His computer had a password that didn't yield to straightforward guesses and Barnes wondered why. Upstairs he heard Knowles moving around with his usual lack of guile. Although Davis was a keen photographer there were no images scattered around the rooms, which might be an indication of the types of photographs taken of course. Barnes went to the bottom of the stairs and yelled.

"Found anything, sir?"

"Not a thing, not one thing out of the ordinary," replied Knowles with a huge hint of exasperation.

"I'll carry on looking," replied Barnes half-heartedly.

"Yeh, do that."

Barnes looked in the kitchen and noted a pile of wood

next to an old stove. Having recently watched a Hercule Poirot mystery on TV, he examined all the pieces of wood at the bottom of the pile to see if any of them were false. There weren't any but it introduced an element of excitement into the otherwise tedious search. He looked in the loose tea leaves for memory sticks and in the biscuit barrel for CDs. With relief he eventually heard Knowles striding downstairs.

"This is strange," said Knowles, picking up a biscuit from the table, "there's nothing wrong here at all – yet we know that Davis was watching other people through binoculars and almost certainly taking pictures too, so where are these pictures?"

"All in complete contrast to Clem Shapiro of course."

"Like chalk and cheese they are."

"Should we take Davis' computer for examination?"

"Absolutely, but I doubt there will be anything on the hard drive; it will be on CDs and what are those thin things called?"

"Memory sticks."

"I need one of those for myself – where would you keep those pervert's things so that you can access them easily, but other people can't?"

"How about his police locker at the station?"

"Good place to start, but perhaps slightly too obvious. Still it should be checked so get the duty sergeant to do it or one of his constables."

"A safety deposit box or a PO box somewhere – do we still have those in Scoresby's main Post Office?"

"Good ideas – I'd prefer a PO box because you can send yourself items through the post and then go and pick them up whenever it suits. Or other people can if you give them the key so that material can be shared and then when you've finished with the materials you can send them back again via the post."

"Especially if you print on labels and don't use handwriting to avoid identifying yourself. Come to think of it…" said Barnes and then walked back into the living room. He came back clutching some labels he'd found by the printer. "…I knew those labels looked odd on their own without any envelopes or packets."

"Post Office box it is then – try Scoresby PO first and see if either Davis, Shapiro, or that Herald woman has a box there – if not you might have to travel further afield. Don't forget they might have been sharing info, so a combination of their names Davis-Shapiro or something equally silly might have been used to book the box."

"Why Herald?"

"She's been seen snooping around suspiciously by both Claude Avon and Danica BC's husband; she's not entirely innocent."

"This place is just too orderly; it's so suspicious – it screams of 'you will never catch me'."

"Well someone did, but not perhaps in the way he imagined."

===========

They drove back to Scoresby station – Barnes went to make enquiries about Davis' locker and boxes for rent in the Post Office.

Knowles went back to his desk, but found a note from the doctor regarding Davis' body and so departed straightaway for the forensics department.

Dr Crabtree looked up as Knowles entered the morgue and smiled; he had some good news, he thought, for the detective inspector.

"Colin, how are you, have you lost weight?"

"I hope so doc, but I only started the diet this morning, so I think it's just a trick of the light as it were. Anyway, what about the shoes and belt we left you – anything of interest?"

"The only evidence is that they were chewed by an animal with fairly sharp teeth. Not surprisingly we also found Clem's fingerprints on the belt and shoes and another set of prints on the shoes."

"Those would have been the Waferr woman's paw prints, I suspect. Do you have any other good news?"

Dr Crabtree breathed in deeply and said, "Well I can tell you that it's the same murderer for both cases. The same amount of force was used, and almost certainly the same weapon, delivered from above, which means I can't tell you anything about the height of the assailant I am afraid, but it does mean that Shapiro was sitting down when he was assaulted."

"Which means that his seat was stolen afterwards by someone – damn they're like vultures here – anyway, does the amount of force indicate a huge amount of strength or a normal amount or...?"

"A strong woman or a moderately strong man hit them both."

"Using a long iron bar or the back of an axe head, an axe with a two-foot long handle?"

"I would say a stone, Colin."

"Not the back of an axe?"

"A stone – blunt and hard - it's easier to wash or dispose of afterwards as well."

"Right, less likely to draw attention to yourself unless people know you're in the Viking society."

"Good point, Colin – there's something odd though about the acorns that were in his mouth. These acorns were deliberately picked from the tree and weren't just loose acorns from the ground, because they were still attached to their casings and had been ripped from the tree, not delicately plucked. Quite a lot of anger involved. Premeditated."

"That's strange because the rhododendron flower had been ripped out of Shapiro's mouth too leaving the stalk, but that occurred after he was dead."

"It seems like these bodies were both visited a number of times before that dog found them."

"Someone made alterations to both crime scenes both before and after that dog found the bodies. Someone was watching all the time and I think I know who it was."

"But would the person watching have also made alterations to the crime scene?"

"I think they did, but after the dog had found the body – that dog drew the watcher's attention to the body, which indicates the watcher wasn't aware of the murder and didn't see who did it. What I am interested in is the person, or persons, who altered the crime scene after the murder and before the dog arrived."

"Well I am glad we sorted that out – did you want to see Davis' internal organs by the way? They're in a bowl over by the sink."

"I don't want to see them thank you, but I'll let Barnesy know – he may be interested in them. You didn't do that just for me did you? You're not upset with me and my lack of enthusiasm to see my ex-colleague's innards?"

"Not at all – it's just a standard process."

"What do you do with them afterwards by the way? Do you stuff them back inside again?"

"We incinerate them, Colin, and you can't have them for Gemma either; that would be unethical."

"She's very choosy about what she eats, so I don't think she'd go for them actually."

Knowles' phone rang and he answered.

"'Allo – Barnesy – we were just talking about you – there's some innards for you here if you want to look… You have some news is that why you rang? Oh right – Davis never worked near Sevenoaks - shame - PO Boxes – you have a list you can share with us – there's no Davis…. nothing obvious for any of them – OK I'll meet you by his locker and see what we can find and then head over to Sharrock Lane to see Greggs and Herald."

Knowles put his phone away and shook Dr Crabtree's hand.

"Thanks, Ben, for the analysis."

"Just doing my job, Colin – take it easy over there in Goat Parva – I sense unfinished business."

===========

After a quick and very late lunch, Knowles met Barnes by Davis' locker. The duty sergeant had found the spare locker key and was eager to see the contents given the rumours that were circulating the station about Davis' demise.

The sergeant waggled the key in the lock and then the locker door opened without a sound.

"Those hinges are well oiled," said Knowles. "I wonder why that is?"

"He didn't want anyone else to be aware that he was going into his locker?"

"Or how often perhaps – he didn't want anyone's attention drawn to this door being opened."

"Perhaps he didn't like squeaky hinges?"

"Yes, perhaps, perhaps he suffered from OCD. Anyway, what do we see in here?"

"Not much," said the duty sergeant in a disappointed manner, "hardly anything."

Inside the locker were a packet of mints, a spare shirt, a spare set of underwear, and an empty glass. There was also a toilet bag containing a razor, toothbrush, toothpaste, and a comb that was completely clean.

"And the cupboard was bare…" murmured Knowles.

Barnes picked up the socks that were rolled into a tight ball and felt them in his hands. He frowned and moved the socks around slightly before unravelling them. A key clicked on the floor and skittered away under the lockers. A constable unwound a paperclip and extricated the key from its temporary resting place. He handed the key to Barnes.

"A Post Office box key, if I am not very much mistaken," said Barnes and was reminded of the list of boxes in his pocket. He pulled the names out. "I wish I knew which of these boxes it belonged to."

Knowles looked down the list: Walker, Smith, Herd, Lucan, Maltravers, Small, Cooke, Savage….

"Sarge, can you get one of your constables to try this key in those PO boxes in the Post Office – get her or him to try those boxes first that belong to people with fancy names like Lucan, Maltravers, Ponsonby, Fortescue-Williams etc.? When a match is found tell the constable to come back and not to touch the contents – I'd like to see whether anyone else comes to that box."

"Right you are, Inspector," said the sergeant and disappeared clutching the list.

"OK, Barnesy, let's head off to Sharrock Lane in Goat Parva and see whether anyone's at home or whether they're all out in the woods watching each other."

Chapter 4

Knowles parked his Land Rover in the car park of the Badger & Ferret Inn and looked at his watch.

"Right, Sergeant Barnes, I think you should go and see Carol Herald and find out what she knows and work out what she's not telling you, if you know what I mean. Above all see if she's the proud owner of a dirty shower curtain or a golf seat that might have been used by her fellow stalkers."

"And you'll be visiting Mr Greggs that Tai Chi artist then?"

"I will – he should be back by now from his job in the big city. I will see you in the tap room when you're finished."

Barnes headed to the left to No 1 Sharrock Lane, while Knowles headed straight over to No 3. A shiny white Mercedes with a warm bonnet was parked in the drive.

Knowles rang the doorbell, stood back slightly and waited. Mr Greggs was perhaps busy after returning from London. After a minute, the door was opened by a slim, brown-haired man wearing tracksuit bottoms who was drying his hair with a blue towel.

"OK, where's the other one, you people usually come in pairs."

"Not a Jehovah's Witness, not happy and smiley enough," said Knowles, brandishing his ID. "The name's Detective Inspector Knowles from Scoresby CID. Can I come in and ask you a few questions about the murder this morning?"

"The murder? What murder? Where? – I didn't see a thing."

Knowles indicated inside with his arm and the two men went indoors.

"Yes, there was a murder in Culpepper's Woods this morning while you were doing your pirouetting and Thai Chee – were you aware that you were being watched?"

"Not at all – although those trees do make me feel like I am the centre of attention and I am aware that there are other people around bird-watching and walking in the woods, but I have never felt like I am being stalked – why would anyone do that?"

"What do you wear when you practice your art?"

"It's a martial art - I wear as little as possible, enough to make me decent I suppose - it would be regarded as skintight by some people."

"That'll be why then – it will show off your curves to good effect."

"That's just creepy – who was murdered and were they watching me?"

"Well, Mr Greggs, you were being watched by at least one person; he…"

"He?"

"…he was called Roger Davis and he was a Police Officer; PC Davis was hit on the head with a blunt instrument while watching you from a convenient location."

"I didn't see anyone carrying a blunt instrument this morning, although I do tend to look straight ahead for between 1 and 2 minutes at a time, so if this murder took place behind me then I wouldn't have seen a thing."

"That's probably what happened in this case. Now you said that you've seen other people walking in the woods and bird-watching – do you know these people's names?"

"I tend not to know too many people here as I work in London of course, but I've seen that Claude guy from the hall. I've seen Mrs Hills and her blessed dog, Barry with his lens, that weird Waferr woman looking for 'things' in the woods, and of course Carol from next door; she heads to work through the woods every morning. I occasionally see Tom Jargoy, but he always looks furtive as though I shouldn't have seen him."

"It would have been easier to ask you who you have not seen."

"It would – I even saw Poppy Avon there once walking with a woman I'd not seen before – I remember Carol said 'hello' to her so she obviously knew her."

45

"And who was bird-watching in your opinion?"

"I thought Claude was and Barry Janus was – because of their long lenses and tripods, but now I just worry that they were photographing me."

"I have no evidence of that but you might be correct. It's possible that other people were watching you and you never saw them."

"That's terrible – still I am not about to change my ways and I will be there tomorrow morning at 6am doing my pirouetting as you put it."

"Where is it you work, Mr Greggs?"

"I work in the Square Mile for a Merchant Bank as a trader."

"Busy at work are you?"

"Oh yes, but no two days are ever the same, Inspector. I have to relax completely before starting the day otherwise my nerves would be fried by lunchtime."

"I can imagine – so why do you live here in Goat Parva when you work there in London; couldn't you live closer?"

"I could do, Inspector Knowles, but it's a complete break to come back here to the lovely countryside and be completely free of the City."

"What's the commute like on a good day?"

"One and a half hours, but with modern wireless technology you can still be working on the train before you get to work."

"Right – it's unfortunate that murder hasn't moved on technologically – people still get bashed over the head and I have to investigate why – there's no App for that."

"Rather you than me, Inspector," said Mr Greggs looking at his iPhone in a slightly bored manner.

"Did you ever see Antonia Avon in the woods or Danica Baker-Clements?"

"I don't know either of them, I have never met them, but I've heard about Danica and her reputation, so if what I have heard is true she wouldn't have time to go for a walk – too busy." Mr Greggs then smiled at the in-joke.

"Indeed, but there was a murder on Tuesday night, the

murder of Clem Shapiro who was watching Danica as she was watching TV."

"Is there a serial killer on the loose, killing stalkers do you think?"

"Possibly but that doesn't fit in with my theory, which isn't completely formed yet in my mind."

At this point Knowles' phone rang.

"'Allo – Barnesy – you're finished? Oh right, well I'll see you over there."

===========

When Knowles headed over to Number 3 Sharrock Lane, Barnes walked along to Number 1, where Carol Herald lived.

He knocked on the front door but there was no reply. Barnes peered through the front windows but it appeared that there was no-one at home. He walked around the side of the house and saw someone digging in the garden. Barnes fought the impulse to see whether it was Carol Herald and just watched for a few moments. He soon saw that it was Reverend Strong from St Timothy's church who seemed to be planting vegetables. After watching for two minutes Barnes finally thought of a suitable question to ask the reverend and so he approached him with some trepidation.

"Reverend Strong, I am Detective Sergeant Barnes from Scoresby CID, I was wondering whether you'd seen Carol Herald recently?"

Reverend Strong finished digging his latest hole and glanced up at Barnes.

"I haven't seen Carol today, but I would expect she'll be back soon unless she's bird-watching in the woods in which case she could be a while yet."

"Thank you – why are you planting vegetables in her garden by the way?"

"Carol's a good friend of the church and we rely on some of our parishioners' gardens to provide food for the events at St Timothy's."

"And what are you planting exactly?"

"I think I should consult my lawyer before answering that question."

"Cannabis?"

"No, Detective Barnes, I was joking, I am planting some carrots and some tomatoes as they are the most popular vegetables with my flock."

"And who are the other parishioners who help with the food provisions?"

"Brenda Jargoy always gives a good head of lettuce, Carly Waferr provides no end of mushrooms, Antonia Avon provides beans and peas and Wendy Jargoy loves growing onions for some reason – she always seems to be crying and I think that might be the reason."

"Wendy Jargoy? Does she still live at home? I thought someone had told me that she'd moved away from Goat Parva?"

"Wendy has issues with her parentage as I am sure you appreciate Detective Barnes. She's not sure who her father really is – Brenda shrugs her shoulders when she's asked that question, which hurts Wendy because it seems as though her mother doesn't care. This isn't the case because Brenda genuinely doesn't know. It could be her husband, Tom, or Lord Avon, or the milkman/postman/plumber – she was apparently involved with them all at the time of conception."

"What, that frumpy middle-aged woman in the village shop who wears those cardies like a prison uniform?"

"That's on the outside, Detective; on the inside is a woman who has been led astray by the forces of the devil incarnate, whose weakness for love has been preyed upon by the angels of Lucifer himself, whose desires for companionship have been taken advantage of by the henchman of hell."

"What is it about women in this village? They're at it all the time with every man who comes their way. I will have to move here I think; all stalkers and loose women."

"Now, Detective, don't be flippant."

"I wasn't being – my village is far too sane for my own good."

"There are some excellent examples of upright, moral women in this village – why think of Antonia Avon."

"She's a drunk who has the attention span of a kitten."

"Carly Waferr then."

"Magic mushrooms from the woods and drinks various potent wines to excess."

"Adelaide Hills?"

"Demented, Reverend Strong – she thinks her dog has stolen her mobile phone when it was recharging and buried it under the azaleas."

"Carol Herald – what have you got against her?"

"Nothing – yet – we haven't met her, but she was in the vicinity when one and possibly two of the murders took place."

"Poppy Avon?"

"Attention span half as long as her mother's – pays for gum using a 50 pound note and then walks off without getting the change because she's talking on the phone to her boyfriend."

"Danica Baker-Clements? Oh no, not a good example to support my theory."

"No, not a good example of a faithful wife."

"I wonder where Carol is – perhaps she had to stay and work late at the animal shelter in Madeley Waterless."

"Does she work on her own over there?"

"No, there are a couple of other volunteers and I think Wendy Jargoy helps out sometimes."

"Who are the other volunteers – do you know their names? We may go over there tomorrow to ask a few questions."

"Oh now this is a memory test – there's the lovely girl called Yasmin, I think and then there's Andrea who is slightly more plain, but they're both beautiful in the eyes of the Lord of course."

"Of course, Reverend – Yasmin and Andrea – I'll make sure I remember those names."

"They look after all sorts of animals – cats, dogs, sheep, pigs, a real menagerie – they're all against animal cruelty especially Yasmin who has a real passion for the subject;

she's been on those protests to the labs where the monkeys and beagles are forced to smoke or wear make-up."

While Reverend Strong was talking Barnes heard some footsteps behind him but when he looked around there was no-one there.

"Was there anyone behind me when you were talking?"

"I didn't see anyone," said Reverend Strong and immediately apologised to his god for telling a little white lie.

"Thank you, Reverend Strong," said Barnes and jogged back to the road. He looked both ways, but saw no sign of anyone. Unbeknownst to him, Barnes was being watched through binoculars, which were trained on him until he disappeared into the Badger & Ferret.

===========

Barnes phoned Knowles from the tap room and then bought him a pint of bitter as well as a pint of lager for himself. He carried them over to a corner table and jotted a few notes down about his conversation with the Reverend Strong.

Knowles blustered in a minute later and downed half his pint before sitting down.

"Thirsty, sir?"

"A bit, but mainly frustrated at how weird this place is – Goat Parva is full of people spying on each other or wandering around in the woods looking for things. What did you find out from Carol Herald?"

"Carol Herald wasn't at home, but I had an interesting conversation with the Reverend Strong about Carol and her contributions to St Timothy's and also about the moral uprightness of the women here."

"More like immoral horizontalness," said Knowles and downed the rest of his drink.

"Another one?" he asked Barnes, who had barely touched his lager.

"Just a half," replied Barnes, "wouldn't want to be breathalysed on the way home."

"I'd deal with that," said Knowles. "Eh, Kev, another pint of bitter and half a lager when you've a minute."

Kevin Spellett, the landlord of the Badger & Ferret, nodded his assent.

"There was something strange that happened – I am 100% certain that whilst he was talking to me someone appeared behind me and yet he denied anyone had been there. I think it might have been Carol Herald."

"So she knew who you were and didn't want to be questioned?"

"It looked that way to me – anyway I found out some useful information about her colleagues at the animal shelter she works at in Madeley."

"Good – we should go there tomorrow to see if she's there – I found out nothing other than Mr Greggs has seen almost everyone in the village at some point during his Tai Chi practice in the woods, even Poppy Avon apparently. They have all been either walking or bird-watching and he's not seen anyone lying on the ground staring at him through binoculars."

Kevin brought over their drinks and placed them on the table.

"Evening officers, on a case?"

"Yeah, we're comparing notes about the two murders here in the past couple of days – do you see much of Carol Herald who lives just over the road?"

"Honestly, no, Inspector Knowles, she doesn't come in here very often other than for the quiz nights and I think she leaves for work very early in the morning from what I've heard – I certainly don't see her during the day."

"Who's in her quiz team, do you know?"

"Well, they always call themselves The Animal Shelter, so I presume that they're Carol's work colleagues. The only other one I partially recognise is Wendy Whatsername from the village shop."

"Wendy Jargoy?" said Barnes.

"That's the one."

"And is there a pretty ginger-haired one and a plainer girl with Carol?"

"Yes, that's about it – that pretty ginger-haired one always objects to any Horse Racing questions, because she says it's cruel."

"Especially if you don't know the answer to the question," quipped Knowles, "that's the cruellest part of all."

"Have you seen anything strange around Goat Parva recently?" said Barnes to Spellett.

"Now you come to mention it," said the landlord and sat down leaning his head conspiratorially forwards so that he could just whisper to them, "I did see something strange – I saw someone walking south along the Leicester Road yesterday morning – they had a jacket on that was similar to the one Clem Shapiro used to wear, so much so that I shouted out to this person thinking it was Clem Shapiro. But it couldn't have been Clem because he was already dead, so who was it? I couldn't tell if it was male or female as they were a couple of hundred yards away."

"And what time was this?" asked Knowles.

"Around 8:30am."

"That fits in with our known timings," said Barnes. "Mrs Hills left the body around 8:15am and then both Carly Waferr and Barry Janus had a look before I arrived around 8:35am. Carly Waferr said the jacket was still there and yet it wasn't there when Barry Janus arrived, so the person walking along the Leicester Road must have been the thief."

"Why walk along the road when you could go into the woods?" asked Knowles.

"Perhaps their vehicle was parked down there around the corner by the gate into Farmer Grant's fields?" said Spellett.

"And they didn't drive back into Goat Parva to your knowledge?"

"Not that I saw – I waited to see whether Clem would drive back through the village, but he didn't."

"It wouldn't have been Clem though – did anyone drive through while you were waiting?"

"Only Poppy Avon in that Ferrari of hers, but she wasn't wearing the jacket I am sure of it – plus the person walking down the road wasn't tottering along on high heels like she does."

"She has a very distinctive walk, but she might have been disguising that just to try and create an illusion," said Knowles, "although I doubt it was her. In any case, no matter who it was it doesn't make any sense – why steal a jacket and then draw attention to yourself in possession of that stolen jacket?"

"Unless you were trying to change the time that the murder took place in people's minds, to give yourself more of an alibi," said Barnes, "but that would only work if the body hadn't been found already. Perhaps the thief hadn't realised that Clem Shapiro's body had already been seen by Adelaide Hills, Carly Waferr, and Barry Janus?"

"Or you were trying to protect the murderer. You steal the jacket, walk down the most public road in Goat Parva wearing that jacket, and hope that people see you and think 'there's Clem Shapiro', and subsequently tell the police that 'I saw Clem Shapiro at 8:30am walking down the Leicester Road' – but then the thief must have known who the murderer was."

"Or have a fair idea."

"Because of something they saw when they were out watching someone?"

"Perhaps you, Kevin, saw Carol Herald walking down the street wearing Clem's jacket and then she headed off to Madeley Waterless through Culpepper's Woods like she normally does. She found Clem after Carly Waferr saw the body, but Carol didn't see Carly because Carol dropped off some produce at St Timothy's and went into the woods via the gate at the back of the cemetery. It's all about timing."

"That's a good theory Barnesy, but why would she continue into Hen's Wood when her work was in the opposite direction?"

"Because she left something in the woods the previous evening when she was watching Danica?"

"Good answer – that could be true – but I am inclined to think that she's quite stupid – she finds the body, steals the jacket, and puts it on because that's what jackets are for and Clem Shapiro isn't going to need it anymore because he's dead."

"And walks down the most public road in Goat Parva?"

"If you're dense that's what you do."

"And she's not protecting anyone?"

"I don't think so, at least not intentionally."

"That's very uncharitable, Inspector," said Spellett, "but I suspect you're correct."

"I think so," replied Knowles, "but I bet she went into Hen's Wood to retrieve something from the previous evening and that does place her very close to the scene of the first murder. We should speak to Carol Herald as soon as possible."

Chapter 5

Carol Herald was in position early for her morning thrills; this morning it was going to be Lord Avon and his stable lad cavorting in the ferns in Hen's Wood. Lord Avon would sit astride the youth and then whip him quite savagely as he bucked and pranced in imitation of a bull – it didn't look much like fun to Carol, but Lord Avon undoubtedly made the lad perform the role until he could take no more.

Carol hid in a low hollow and peered through the undergrowth until she saw the two males approaching. She readied her zoom lens and checked the video worked correctly. Presently, Lord Avon pushed the youth onto his haunches and mounted him roughly. A fox or badger scurried through the bracken to her right.

Lord Avon started shouting "Ye haaa, ride 'em cowboy, ye haa." The youth jumped up and down slightly but with no enthusiasm whatsoever. As Carol Herald was about to press play the blunt instrument came down on her skull and caused her to lose consciousness forever.

In the background Lord Avon's, "Ye haaas" could be heard above the pleas from the stable hand for him to stop. The assailant whispered, "No more animals for you to hurt" into Carol's unhearing ear and crawled off into the woods.

===========

Mrs Hills collected Bingo from his doghouse and they walked happily along Sharrock Lane avoiding both Culpepper's Woods and Doggett's Field, which were both still cordoned off because of the two recent murders. Bingo ran along chasing the occasional pheasant and barking at the geese by the river. They walked along the bank and entered Hen's Wood by the gate at the corner of Doggett's Field.

Almost immediately Mrs Hills saw Barry Janus taking a picture of the river with the leaves of the trees hanging prettily over the slate-grey water.

"Good morning, Barry," said Mrs Hills, "nice weather for photography, isn't it?"

"It most certainly is," said Barry lining up another image. "I've only been here five minutes and I've taken a good half dozen images already."

"It's about the only place we could go for a walk this morning, what with the police having cordoned off the woods and field over there."

"What's that your dog's got in his mouth?"

Mrs Hills froze and slowly turned her head to see Bingo carrying a stick in his mouth.

"Oh thank goodness for that," said Mrs Hills, "I was wondering what item of clothing he would have brought back this morning."

Barry Janus furrowed his brow – he wasn't sure what she meant.

She picked up the stick and threw it into the woods and Bingo retrieved it. She threw it again and Bingo fetched it once more. She threw it again and Bingo disappeared after it. Mrs Hills began to relax and smiled for the first time in two days – this was just like the old times. She turned around and saw Bingo heading towards her carrying a scarf, which he dumped at her feet before turning around and returning to the undergrowth.

Mrs Hills barely suppressed a scream as Bingo came back with a glasses case wedged in his mouth.

"Drop it, drop it immediately," shrieked Mrs Hills. "Oh no, who is it this time?"

"What's happened," said Barry Janus, "what's he done?"

"He's not done anything other than appear to have found yet another body, which he's started to strip as with the other two finds."

"Bingo found the other two bodies too? That must have been upsetting."

Mrs Hills grabbed Bingo's lead and allowed herself to be led into the woods by her retriever.

After twenty seconds Barry Janus heard a loud, "Oh God, not another one" and hurried off to where the sound came from. He soon saw Mrs Hills bent double, crying her eyes out, and pulling her hair. She soon composed herself – this wasn't half as bad as the camel in the desert in Morocco – and walked off through the woods towards St Timothy's church. Barry retreated to his tripod, took another quick snap, and then headed home. He had seen the body and realised he was now the only one of them left. He feared for his life and would stay at home in Goat Parva for the rest of the day other than to make a quick trip out to Scoresby – it was his turn today after all.

============

Knowles was playing string with Gemma when his mobile phone rang.

"'Allo, Knowles here – oh it's you, Barnesy – what do you mean am I sitting down? I should sit down – another body near the river in Hen's Wood – almost certainly Carol Herald. Oh damnation, and I will know who found her – that bastard dog. What did it take this time? Is there anything in her mouth? Well leave it to forensics to see. No, you deal with them this time – I will see you at Mrs Hills' house in about an hour."

Knowles picked up the string and dangled it in front of Gemma's nose– she aimed a couple of meaty left hooks at it, followed by a straight right, which shredded the strands into small pieces.

How symbolic of this case, thought Knowles, *just when you think you have strung together a coherent theory the whole thing comes apart in your hands.*

Gemma looked dismissively at the remains of the string in her paw and walked off to see whether any tasty food had magically appeared in her bowl. She didn't appreciate her staff going on non-meat diets as she couldn't abide toast, carrots, or bananas.

Knowles looked at Gemma and wondered where the case would be if Adelaide Hills had owned a cat. Or a hamster.

Anything but that eager retriever. Still Bingo had indirectly made the police realise that more people had seen the body than had currently come forward to tell them so. This must mean they had something to hide or were just plain embarrassed to show the police what they had been up to in the early morning.

On the other hand hamsters don't steal mobile phones when they're recharging or interfere with crime scenes. Knowles' phone rang again – it was the duty sergeant.

"Inspector Knowles, Constable Smythe's found a match for that key found in Davis' locker – the box was in the name of Maltravers – figure that out – what do you want us to do?"

"Well, Sarge, I would like a plain clothes officer to watch that box all day today and to follow anyone who goes and opens it. The officer should just follow them mind you and find out where they go – don't make an arrest just yet – that's if someone turns up at all - my main suspect has just been found dead in Hen's Wood. Any questions, Sarge?"

"No – that's clear enough, Inspector – thank you."

Knowles went over to his computer and typed 'Maltravers' into his search engine. The third entry's headline read,

Maltravers Herald of Arms Extraordinary is a current officer of arms extraordinary in England. As such, *Maltravers* is a royal herald...

"Maltravers a type of Herald – clever I suppose," said Knowles to himself, "oh Carol, why did you avoid being seen by Barnes last night? You might still be alive."

Knowles thought about the best way to proceed with the investigation – first of all they should go and visit Mrs Hills again, then enter Carol Herald's house and see what was there, and finally go to the animal shelter in Madeley Waterless. The three murdered people must have a connection other than the fact that they stalked people as a hobby. His thoughts turned to whom could possibly be killed next given that Barry Janus, Claude Avon, Tom Jargoy, Poppy Avon, and some unknown friend of Carol Herald's had all been seen in various suspicious locations.

Knowles pondered the possibilities until it was time to go to his now customary daily conversation with Mrs Adelaide Hills.

==========

Barnes was removing an imaginary speck of dirt from the bonnet of his gleaming Morgan sports car as Knowles arrived outside The Cottage in his not so shiny Land Rover.

"Do you have a sense of déjà vu, sir?" quipped Barnes as Knowles extricated himself with difficulty from his vehicle – surely this diet couldn't be making him fatter could it?

"Yes, it's déjà vu all over again," said Knowles spying Mrs Hills looking at them through the lace curtains in her kitchen. "I wonder what the dog took this time."

"I got the impression that the body this morning had not been disturbed."

"Interesting – I look forward to seeing Carol's house later on this morning. Perhaps she was more involved than we thought."

Barnes knocked on the front door and Mrs Hills took an age before opening it.

"Good morning, Inspector Knowles and Sergeant Barnes – I wonder why you're here?"

"Another day, another murder, Mrs Hills, and another body for your dog to find," said Knowles as they headed to the kitchen.

"Yes, it seems that way doesn't it? Bingo seems to have a homing instinct for the bodies that people leave lying around."

"It's not people, Mrs Hills, Adelaide sorry, it's one person."

"Can you be so sure, Inspector?"

"I think so. I thought Carol Herald might have done the first two murders, but she can't have hit herself over the head and thrown the weapon away before hitting the ground, so I have eliminated her from my enquiries."

Barnes asked a question. "Can you describe what happened this morning, Mrs Hills, in your own words?"

"We couldn't go to Doggett's Field or Culpepper's Woods because of the previous murders, so we walked along the river bank, saw Barry Janus taking pictures of the river, and then I started playing fetch with Bingo. Unfortunately, the third time he didn't bring the stick back, but a scarf instead and then a glasses case."

"Did you leave Barry alone with the body?"

"I had to, to report the body to the police, to yourselves," and Mrs Hills spread her arms wide as though to embrace them both.

"I think tomorrow when you go for your walk you should have a police escort, so that you don't have to leave the scene of the crime and allow other people to interfere with the body."

"You are joking, Inspector – you've cordoned everywhere off so there isn't anywhere for us to walk now, except along the road southwards and then we can cut into Culpepper's Woods that way via the stile."

"Are you making a prediction of where the next body will be found, Adelaide?"

"Don't be ridiculous, Inspector, it's the only place left."

"You could walk south along the river, Adelaide."

"Bingo likes the woods and he does tend to jump into the water whenever he can so I avoid the river if at all possible."

"Does he retrieve things from the river – fish for example? Old prams? Tyres?"

"No, Inspector, he doesn't," replied Mrs Hills rather testily.

"In all seriousness, Adelaide, there will be a WPC outside your house at 7:30am tomorrow morning, so she can escort you on your walk."

"But that will be so embarrassing won't it – what will people think?"

"What does it matter what they think, Adelaide?"

"They may think I am out on probation from an open prison and need guarding."

"They know you have nothing to do with the murders, so there's no need to fret," concluded Knowles. "Anyway, I should be going as I have to go and see Carol Herald's house on Sharrock Lane. Don't forget if you think of anything else, do give me a call. Where's Bingo by the way?"

"He's outside in the doghouse; I scolded him again this morning for finding yet another body and he rather took it to heart."

"Is he regretting being a retriever do you think – perhaps he'd prefer to be a pointer or an Alsatian?"

"He can't regret his own nature – dogs don't have the power of reason do they? Besides if he was a pointer he'd still find the body and point at it until someone saw him. I am not sure what an Alsatian would do."

"Bark lots in my experience – that's why I can't stand dogs – all that noise to draw attention to themselves and so many needs it's untrue. Anyway, poor Bingo will just have to be a proud retriever won't he – have you had him long?"

"I've had him since he was three months old. I got him from the animal shelter where Carol Herald works or used to work at least. It's amazing how the conversation has come nearly full circle."

Barnes smiled reassuringly at Mrs Hills as the police officers left the kitchen and returned to their vehicle. They drove down to the car park on Doggett's Field and then walked back to 1, Sharrock Lane. Once again the Forensics team had done a thorough job without disturbing much inside the house.

The walls of Carol Herald's front room were covered in pictures of trees and forests, almost all of them in black and white. Forensics had left the computer on so that Knowles and Barnes could see the contents of all her disk drives – apparently there was no password set, so she obviously didn't have anything to hide.

"I'd just like to check to see whether Carol had used Photoshop recently," said Barnes looking on her desktop for the program icon, "I have a theory about what was happening here."

Eventually he found the program and loaded it.

"Let's see what she was looking at recently," said Barnes, checking the most recent files opened by the program. "There you are – all of the images were viewed from the CD/DVD drive and the file names were just dates; very recent dates and always in the same yyyy-mm-dd format."

"That's very good detective work, Sergeant, but I would guess we will not find those disks here as they will have been posted back to the PO box already."

"And I would guess we will find some small jiffy bags and printed labels in a hidden place."

"Did you notice, Barnesy that the last two files she looked at were dated Tuesday and Wednesday – I wonder what those images were – and I wonder whether the date refers to the processing date or the date the images were taken."

"Probably the date the pictures were taken – so perhaps Tuesday's images were taken at night at the Baker-Clements' house, but where were Wednesday's taken I wonder? Wherever it was nobody was murdered then as PC Davis was killed on Thursday morning."

"Right, Barnesy – if we can find out where Wednesday's stalkers met then we can better understand why three particular people got bashed on the head."

"Sir, do you think they all attend every single stalking session and then share the photographs afterwards or do you think they take it in turns to stalk?"

"I would say they surround the subject of their attentions and then snap away or video and breathe heavily of course and then share the pictures afterwards."

"They mostly live in separate villages and post the disks at different post offices or boxes, so that they don't raise any suspicions by sending packets to the same PO box from the same Post Office."

"What I wonder, Barnesy, is whether there were just three of them and they're all now dead or whether there was a fourth person, who either killed the others or is going to be the next to die. It's going to be a difficult decision to make if someone turns up at the PO box today – do we arrest them on suspicion of murder or take them into police protection?"

"Take them in for further questioning and while we are questioning them slowly, we find out the contents of that box and see what kind of images were being shared around the stalking community of Goat Parva."

"We await that call – in the interim let's check the rest of her humble abode and see what's around – I feel lighter today so I will head upstairs and see what the bedrooms reveal."

"And I will stay downstairs and look for those packets and labels."

Knowles huffed and puffed up the stairs and started in the bathroom where he made a note of the shower curtain – it looked new and had never been used by someone to lie on in the woods. He checked in the cupboards and then moved to the bedrooms where he searched under the beds and looked through Carol's large collection of jeans and t-shirts in her closet and wardrobes. Everything was in order and there were no images of any kind to be seen. He looked in the landing basket and just found 1 item of dirty clothing – a jumper that had seen better days and was obviously used to handle cats and dogs that were moulting.

Meanwhile Barnes looked in the kitchen and dining room, even taking apart a photo of Carol's family to see if there was a secret letter hidden in the back, as had been the case in a recent episode of a particularly enjoyable crime caper. The lounge was well hoovered and not a cushion was out of place on the settee. It began to remind Barnes of PC Davis' home – it was almost as though she was expecting to be searched.

Knowles came down the stairs looking very disappointed and asked Barnes,

"Do we have a key for her shed – there's nothing up there at all?"

"Nor down here, sir, just like Davis' house." Barnes looked in the kitchen at the keys on the rack and chose the longest key he could find. He went outside and then came back and took the rest, but none of them worked.

"None of them work, sir, so we will have to improvise won't we?"

"Absolutely, Barnesy, what would you recommend?"

"I think the spade that Reverend Strong was using last night, which he didn't put away, and is still leaning against the wall out there."

"Carol, old neat and tidy Carol, must have missed that when she came home in the dark."

"If she'd talked to me instead of running away then she might be alive."

Knowles nodded and then went outside and grabbed the spade. He lifted it up and brought it down heavily on the shed lock four times splintering the wood sufficiently for the lock to be levered off.

Barnes opened the door and switched on the shed light. Around the walls neatly arranged were all the garden tools you could ever need from trowels to hoes from strimmers to forks. Of more interest was the central table, over which was spread a shower curtain that had seen better days and was stained with mud, old leaves, and chlorophyll from crushed plants. Barnes looked on the shelf under the table and pulled out some jiffy bags and labels. Barnes smiled and placed them into a plastic bag he obtained from his jacket pocket – a trick he had learnt from Knowles.

"That's one of the items I was expecting," said Knowles pointing at the curtain, "now let's see if we can find the other one – it might be hanging up or it could be in a rucksack."

"There's a small ledge up there," said Barnes and stood on the table to reach into the shed's roof space – his hand encountered something and he brought it down and placed it on the table. The small, camouflaged rucksack looked as though it was well used.

They both stared at it for a few moments as though this could be a significant occasion – eventually Knowles gingerly unzipped the outer pocket and smiled at the contents. Neatly folded inside was Clem Shapiro's leather jacket, thinner than he thought it would be, but still the leather jacket he wanted to see.

"Barnesy, phone Forensics, and get them over here straightaway – we should get these two items examined so we can be 100% sure their original owners are who we think they are."

Barnes went out of the shed to make the call and Knowles unzipped all the rucksack's pockets and carefully let all the contents fall onto the shower curtain. There was an old apple core, a torch, and a black wool hat, as well as the jacket. All that was apparently needed for a night's stalking in Goat Parva. There was also a stem from a flower.

Knowles went out into the morning sunshine and stood looking out towards the fast-flowing river. His head was spinning with what these discoveries meant. Clem Shapiro's golf seat was not in the shed, so presumably Carol Herald hadn't taken that item because someone else, perhaps the murderer, had already taken it. What this did mean was that Carol Herald had been close at hand when both murders had taken place – is that why she was killed – she saw something she shouldn't have? If she was in league with Shapiro and Davis in a stalking group then she showed absolutely no remorse at their demise – she didn't report their deaths and took items from them that would make her own stalking activities more comfortable in the future. How cold was that – how unfeeling could someone be?

"Forensics are on their way, sir," said Barnes and then he pointed at the shed. "We didn't find that golf seat in there did we?"

"I didn't think we would, Barnesy, I didn't think we would. Carol Herald is a very neat and well ordered person by all accounts and she wouldn't have murdered someone and then come back seven hours later to steal their jacket – she would have done it at the time of the murder."

"Just so I can get this straight in my mind then – Mrs Hills and that dog of hers find Clem Shapiro's body on Wednesday morning and then she goes off to report the body. Then Carly Waferr looks at the body, and then Carol Herald steals the jacket before Barry Janus sees the body and before I arrive. She then heads down the Leicester Road where she is seen by Kevin Spellett. That means she must have been in the vicinity when Mrs Hills and the others were looking at the body and she was waiting to get the jacket."

"That's correct – Claude Avon verified that last fact when we interviewed him; he said he got a good view of her that morning but not on the morning he was in the woods when Davis was murdered."

"But how did Carol know there was a jacket on a dead body in a rhodo bush in the Baker-Clements' garden?"

"I can only think that she didn't know for sure – if she's in a stalking club with Shapiro and Davis and others then they probably arrange to stalk collectively and share their photos, videos etc later on. They take different spots around the stalking victim and know where each of the others is; presumably if Carol phoned Clem and there was no reply she'd go back to the scene of the stalk and find him dead, taking his jacket when there was a moment between all the visitors."

"Would Bingo have sensed her presence?"

"He might have but there were many other distractions for our beloved Bingo to cope with. Oh, one other thing, I found part of a stalk from a flower in the rucksack. How neat is that of Carol? She must have removed it to spare Clem's afterlife blushes and taken it with her, not realising there was still part of the stalk in his mouth."

"The timing is amazing then – she must have removed the flower first, because no one mentioned a flower at all, not Barry, not Carly, not Mrs Hills. Carol must have removed the flower and then heard Bingo the dog and hid until Mrs Hills, Bingo, and Carly Waferr left and then she took the jacket before Barry Janus arrived. Timing is everything – she must have really wanted that jacket."

"Indeed, Barnesy, she was determined to have that jacket."

"That's obsessive compulsive behaviour, sir," said Barnes shaking his head. "So what happened on the Thursday morning in Culpepper's Woods? Davis gets smacked on the head but Herald knows where he's lying, so she waits for Mrs Hills to leave and then steals the shower curtain the body was lying on without a second thought as to the fact that Davis is dead."

"I think that's it - I wonder if she was wearing her rucksack that morning; it would make it easier to hide the shower curtain than if she was carrying it around in her hand."

"That's something to ask Claude Avon isn't it? We should pay him another visit. Soon."

"I hope that the three people who've been murdered aren't

the only ones in the stalking group otherwise this could be a difficult case to solve. Danica BC said she was watched by three people on Tuesdays so might these three bodies be those people?"

"I should revisit her and ask her to verify how many people are watching her next Tuesday."

"I thought you'd be keen to revisit her – I am not letting you go on your own, young Mr Barnes, she'd be too much for you."

"What about this theory – the three bodies are those stalkers and Danica's inappropriately named husband Roger isn't in America at all, but is instead in a caravan in the deepest woods and is killing off all the people who are watching his wife?"

"As opposed to all the people who are giving his wife a good time in their own home? That doesn't really work for me."

The vehicle of the Forensics team pulled into the drive.

"Good point, sir – oh when I spoke to Forensics earlier they confirmed that the same murder weapon had been used on Carol Herald as with the others."

"Right - if there are other members of the stalking group they must be very worried by now because they could be next – as they've arrived I think it's time to go to the animal shelter in Madeley Waterless."

Barnes showed the Forensics people the items they should examine for possible clues about who'd used the items and when. Barnes and Knowles then walked back to the car parked by Doggett's Field and headed over to Madeley.

============

The animal shelter was at the opposite end of the village from Davis' house. Barnes drove into the parking area and chose a spot by the entrance. People were milling about carrying puppies, kittens, and rabbits.

"Who's in charge here, Barnesy?"

"I am not sure that anyone is – it's a sort of collective, cooperative type arrangement, so we could ask for Yasmin, Andrea, or Wendy I suppose."

"Looks like business as usual doesn't it? They're not closed to commemorate Carol's passing."

"They're certainly not – perhaps it's what Carol would have wanted."

"Perhaps it is – let's see what we can learn."

They both got out of the vehicle and headed to what looked like reception. There was a till but it seemed like all of the staff was busy helping their customers find the right animal for their situation.

Barnes and Knowles both looked closely at everyone to see whether any identification badges were being used or whether staff wore a t-shirt that would identify them to visitors.

"There's an Andrea over there," said Knowles.

"Which one?"

"The girl with the green t-shirt who looks quite plain."

"And there's Wendy Jargoy. I recognise her – she looks like she's just peeled an onion as usual."

"Right you take Wendy, Barnesy, and I'll try and speak to Andrea – she looks a bit rough to me."

Barnes nodded and headed off to speak to Wendy Jargoy.

Just in case the conversation didn't go well, Knowles thought of some cat related questions – why do cats eat grass to make themselves sick? Why do cats always try and trip you up on the stairs? Why do cats ignore the TV when they are so inquisitive about everything else? – and headed over towards Andrea, who had just finished helping a young mother with her questions about her daughter's fish.

"Andrea? My name is Inspector Knowles from Scoresby CID – do you have a few moments to talk?"

"It's about Carol, right?" said Andrea, "Carol Herald?"

"It is, yes, did you know her well?"

"I worked with her and went to some pub quizzes with her, so I know she knew a lot about geography and English History, but that's about it."

"Did she like animals?"

"Indeed she did, Inspector, but she was a bit rough with

some of the larger dogs and I know that Yasmin didn't like her treatment of them."

"Is Yasmin here today, so we can speak to her too?"

"We, Inspector?"

"Yes, my sergeant, Barnesy as I call him, is speaking to Wendy at the moment."

"Yasmin has her designated day off today, Inspector, so she won't be in until tomorrow – perhaps you could come back then?"

"You don't seem that upset about Carol Herald being murdered, Andrea."

"Inspector Knowles, we have to put down animals here every day or two because of their brutal treatment by human beings, so we work in a situation where death is ever present – it's upsetting about Carol, but life has to go on."

"But Carol wasn't put down was she? You put down animals for their own good – because you don't want them to suffer any more, you don't want them to experience more pain; Carol was murdered in the prime of her life for reasons I haven't worked out yet, but I will do. Where were you this morning by the way, around 7am?"

"I was at home in Scoresby and nobody can verify that because I live alone – I resent the question because I loved working with Carol and would never harm her."

"I ask everyone that question, well most people anyway; do you know where Yasmin lives?"

"Yasmin lives in Frixton with her boyfriend."

"She'll be in work tomorrow, so we can visit her then?"

"Yes, Inspector, we're only allowed one day off at a time."

"Did Carol get on with everyone at the animal shelter?"

"She got on with the staff of course, but she did have a few disputes with people who she thought were mistreating their animals; we all come across cases like that, but Carol used to shout and yell at some people and I am sure they resented it, especially as it was in front of other people."

"You wouldn't happen to know who these people were?"

"Well, I know that one of them was the daughter of Lord Avon – Poppy Avon - and that she mistreated her miniature poodle by dying its fur and also feeding it a starvation diet, so that it was really thin – she then had the temerity to complain that we'd sold her a sick dog. Well Carol gave her a real mouthful in return and Poppy threw the dog at her and told her to keep it and that she'd be revenged for this public embarrassment."

"And when was this, Andrea?"

"About three months ago."

"Thank you – and can you remember any other people with whom Carol had arguments?"

"There was the butcher and his assistant Clem Shapiro; Carol hated the way they used to treat their animals, killing them without any dignity at all. She also argued with Mr Greggs, because he wanted a dog and she told him it would be cruel on the dog because he was out at work all day and the dog would have no company."

"How did Shapiro and Greggs react to this?"

"They weren't happy bunnies as it were, but Shapiro just ignored her advice and I believe that Greggs bought a dog from the pet shop in Scoresby."

"Really? I didn't see one or see any evidence of one even when I visited him."

"Perhaps I am wrong then, but that's what I heard."

"Who told you – can you remember?"

"I think Yasmin told me that she'd seen him in there one day."

"Right - something else to ask her tomorrow."

At that moment Knowles noticed Barnes had finished speaking to Wendy Jargoy and decided that he'd spoken to Andrea for long enough.

"Anyway, thank you for your time, Andrea, we should be getting along with our investigations."

He walked over to Barnes who was scribbling furiously in his notebook trying to remember everything that Wendy had told him.

"So, Sergeant what did she say?"

"Wendy was quite forthcoming – apparently Yasmin is on her designated holiday today but will be in tomorrow. It seems as though everyone loved Carol and the work she did at the animal shelter, but Carol did have arguments with some customers who she thought mistreated their animals."

"Is that right?"

"Yes, apparently Carol argued with PC Davis about his dog and the way he treated it out in the woods, whipping it with branches from oak trees."

"No!"

"And Carol argued with Poppy Avon about her miniature poodle and the fact she dyed it green."

"That's it – no argument with Clem Shapiro or Mr Greggs the merchant banker?"

"Wendy didn't mention anyone else in particular, but there were other customers Carol argued with, but Wendy didn't think they were local."

"I see – well I was told about Poppy Avon too, so that's interesting – I was also told that Carol argued with Clem Shapiro and Mr Greggs; Shapiro because he was a butcher and Greggs because he wanted to buy a dog that he would leave at home all day."

"That would be cruel though, leaving a dog at home all day sad and lonely without any company."

"My Gemma can handle it, but then she's a cat that can take itself for a walk."

"Has there been an element of collusion here do you think, sir?"

"I think so, but I am not sure why, because they'd know that we'd talk afterwards and find out the similarities between their stories. There's been an attempt to muddy the waters most certainly, but we could end up second guessing ourselves here, so we should investigate these various stories as best we can."

"When we went to Davis' house there was no evidence of a dog whatsoever – not even a water bowl outside or scratching by the backdoor."

"Right, just like there was no evidence of a dog at Mr Greggs' house. Anyway, we should head back to the station and write these reports."

===========

As the two officers left the car park Andrea walked over to Wendy Jargoy.

"Did you tell them what we agreed?"

"Of course I did, Andrea. We've certainly given them something to think about for a few days – I wonder where Yasmin is today, she's supposed to be here isn't she - not on holiday."

"She was probably on animal patrol last night at one of the large research establishments that we both know she visits periodically to see how much cruelty is being inflicted in the name of science."

"Is that where she went a couple of nights ago when she cut her hand on the barbed wire?"

"Tuesdays are one of her regular nights to try and break into those places."

"What would happen if she got caught?"

"She wouldn't get caught, Wendy – you've seen the police in action just now with Laurel and Hardy, or whatever their names were. They don't have a clue what's going on."

"They aren't as stupid as you think, Andrea."

"We'll see about that, Wendy, we'll see about that."

==========

Knowles and Barnes were at that moment comparing notes as they drove back to Scoresby.

"So, Sergeant Barnes, were your suspicions aroused by the similarity of their stories or do you think women just gossip a lot and so their evidence will be similar?"

"Both, sir, but mainly the former – it will be interesting to speak to Yasmin and see which of the other two she most apes in her evidence – my money's on Andrea as she's quite a controlling character I think."

"Exactly right, Barnesy, but the skilful part is that there's elements of truth interwoven through their stories and the scary thing is that some of what they say is probably true – for example Davis beating his dog in the woods with oak branches – is that why someone cruelly placed seven acorns in his mouth? One for each lash of his poor dog? Is that why the acorns were torn from the tree and not just picked up from the forest floor?"

"So Carol knew that Davis mistreated his dog and berated him, but so many other people saw her doing this that all those people would know too."

"Just like they'd know that she verbally abused Clem Shapiro because she did that in front of everyone."

"And yet, and yet, they were probably in the same stalking club together – so was that argument just a cover for their nocturnal activities?"

"Who knows now, Sergeant; I have no idea when that argument took place - it might have been last month or last year. Andrea didn't mention a time."

Barnes' phone suddenly started ringing – it was the duty sergeant.

"DS Barnes, Robinson has been watching the PO box in the Post Office and it seems like someone is circling around and may be going to open the box very soon."

"He's got his orders, just follow the person who opens the box and don't attempt an arrest – make sure no police are in the vicinity and keep all sirens off. We want the collector to think that everything has gone well."

Barnes reported the progress to Knowles who smiled with some relief.

"So they're not all dead then – there's at least one left and it will be interesting to see who it is – they will have some very awkward questions to answer and will be the main suspect in the three murders."

"So why would the two girls make up stories about Carol Herald if they weren't true? To try and throw us of their scent?"

"That's quite possible, but it might be to disguise the fact they didn't like her. If they both tell us that Carol argued with other people then it doesn't make them look so bad in our eyes when we eventually find out they argued with Carol too."

"Where do you think Yasmin was, sir?"

"Not on a planned day's holiday that's for sure – you saw how busy they were – they needed someone else's help. If that'd been me and one of my colleagues had been killed I'd have been in work and talking to people to see how they were coping with her loss."

"Perhaps they couldn't get a hold of her?"

"That's probably true – but I wonder why that is? Perhaps her mobile phone is switched off or it's recharging."

"Perhaps Bingo stole her phone too - just for practice."

"That bastard dog's involved in this somehow, but I don't know why I think that."

"In an indirect way though, sir?"

"Of course, but what would draw that dog to those bodies – it's a thieving canine that's for sure, but what else is there?"

Barnes' phone rang again.

"Right - a definite pick up of some packets from the PO box and the suspect has placed them in his camera bag and has headed out of the Post Office….he's being tailed by two teams….heading towards the Goats public house. OK, leave him well alone until he's in his domicile wherever that is."

"It's a he, Sergeant, and it's not Bingo by the sound of it, which is a huge relief."

"With a camera bag?"

"Could be anyone then."

"In which case, they might be heading our way, so shouldn't we get off the road so they don't recognise us?"

"Yes, good spotting, Sergeant Barnes, let's pull into the car park at the Drover's Arms and watch the road from behind the hedge – that takes me back to when I worked on the team that enforced speed limits; that was our favourite place to catch speeding drivers as they couldn't see us, but we could see them of course."

"Did you enjoy that, sir?"

"I did, especially when I caught some young man driving his sports car far too fast for the road conditions and without due care and attention."

"Did you used to play snooker?"

"No, not enough red cars around here, but they did play that on the M1 further south until the Chief Constable asked why no yellow or white cars were ever stopped."

Barnes and Knowles waited for a few minutes and then a flash of red flew by them – Poppy Avon's Ferrari.

"Was that Claude in there or Poppy?"

"That was Poppy Avon, Barnesy, and on the front seat was a purple coloured animal, perhaps a dog of some description."

"Not Claude?"

"Not Claude. Oh ho, who do we have here in that dirty brown van?"

"Carly Waferr. I didn't even know she drove a car?"

"Don't tell me they've all been to Scoresby this morning – this isn't possible."

"And here's Tom Jargoy in another dirty brown van."

Barnes phoned the duty sergeant.

"Hi, Sarge, where's Robinson?... He's on the road to Goat Parva following a brown van – which one? Is he sure about that? We've just seen two others go by. OK."

"Thirty seconds, sir," said Barnes and crouched down by the road.

About a minute later another brown van came chugging around the corner followed at a discreet distance by Robinson's unmarked police car. Knowles and Barnes had been tying imaginary shoelaces, which in Barnes' case was highly suspect because if anyone had checked they would have seen he was wearing Wellington boots.

"Who was it, did you see, sir?"

"I was keeping my head down, Sergeant."

"Shall we chase after them?"

"Let's just wait until the brown van has reached its home base."

After two minutes Barnes' phone rang again.

"Robinson's in Goat Parva, by the Post Box, waiting for us."

They jumped in their vehicle and headed to the village. Parking in front of the shop they saw Robinson standing by his vehicle and motioned him over to them.

"Where did it go, the brown van?"

"First house in the village on the right hand side of the road, next to the church."

"You sure it's the correct brown van, because we saw three?"

"I only saw one brown van and it's parked in the drive of that house."

75

"Right, let's go," said Knowles, "let's see who this is…"

The three men jogged, or in Knowles' case, ambled down the path, past the shop and Mrs Hills' house, before crossing Leicester Road in front of St Timothy's church.

"When we go into the drive, you go round the back, Barnesy, and you, Constable, stay out of sight behind the van in case he tries to make a run for it."

The three men sneaked into the drive. The van was parked there. Knowles touched the bonnet, which was hot. Robinson stayed in the shadows and Barnes worked his way through the overgrown garden to the back of the house. After 1 minute Knowles knocked on the front door.

There was no movement inside – so Knowles shouted through the letter box,

"Come out, come out whoever you are. We know you're in there."

He tried the front door, which was locked. He radioed Barnes at the back of the house – he'd seen nothing, so Knowles asked him to make an entry via the back door.

Knowles heard the smashing of glass and a figure came running towards the front door, unlocked it, and tripped over Knowles' outstretched foot.

"Oh yes and where are you going in such a hurry?"

Barry Janus stared back at him and smiled.

"Inspector Knowles, what a pleasant surprise. I thought they'd come to kill me."

Chapter 6

Friday, afternoon

Barry Janus sat in Interview Room Number 1 at Scoresby Police Station and relief flowed through his veins – he had genuinely believed his life was in danger, but he wasn't quite sure who from – the person or people who'd committed three murders so far were unknown to him, but he was convinced that he would be next. He just hoped that the police didn't think that he'd killed anyone. He had been looking forward to seeing the latest images from the others although he wasn't sure what to do with the DVDs now that he was the only one left – could the group carry on with just one person or should he try and find some new members, who were interested in the nocturnal habits of the good folks of Goat Parva?

Detective Inspector Knowles came into the room and nodded to the constable. Knowles smiled as he sat down opposite Barry Janus.

"Barry, my lad, I have to congratulate you on the quality of the images – someone obviously has a photographer's eye. Sergeant Barnes will be with us in a minute – he's just having a cold shower."

"They're not my images, Inspector they're mainly Carol's and Roger's photos with some of Clem's."

"You only had one DVD, so is that PO box full of other DVDs from all your previous stalking sessions?"

"Only about 3 month's worth – that's how long we've been together and using this drop box idea."

"The images on the DVD were from when exactly?"

"From Monday night when Roger was watching Danica Baker-Clements and Tuesday morning when Carol was watching Lord Avon and his stable lad."

"That's interesting because both their cameras contained no images when they were killed, so why would that be?"

"Because they'd have transferred all the images to the DVDs directly and then deleted the images on the camera's card, just for security reasons."

"Security reasons – your security or the security of the people in the images?"

"Ours."

"When we were at your house earlier, who did you think we were and why would whoever you thought we were be trying to kill you?"

"Because the other three members of the group have been killed and I assumed you were intending to make it four. I have no idea who has killed the others but I assume that I will be next."

At that moment there was a knock at the door and Sergeant Barnes came into the room.

"Alright, Barnesy, you've calmed down have you?" Knowles then turned to Barry Janus and continued, "He was most impressed by the images of Danica being taken from behind – any idea who the person was? For some reason the camera wasn't focused on him."

"With her it could literally be anyone in the county – she's not choosy."

"So, Barry, now that Sergeant Barnes is here can you explain to us why we should not consider you suspect number one for the murders of your fellow stalkers?"

"Why would I do that; why would I murder three people?"

"Because you wanted to keep the DVDs all for yourself; perhaps the others wanted to stop the stalking and you wouldn't hear of it and there was a big argument and you decided to knock them on the head."

"Do you seriously think I would murder Carol Herald and then wait around for Adelaide Hills and her dog to see me near the crime scene?"

"You might not be very bright, Barry."

Barnes asked a question. "Where were you, Barry, on Tuesday night?"

"I was in the rhododendron bushes in Danica Baker-Clements' garden, but on the Hen's Wood side not the

Doggett's Field side – there's a path from my back garden into the woods and it only took five minutes to get there."

"And you didn't see anyone else?"

"I saw all the others in their usual spots with lenses and binoculars…"

"The others being?"

"Carol, Roger, and Clem, but there was someone else on the Doggett's Field side I am sure because I saw a figure walking away towards the river path just before the postman came down the drive to visit Danica, her third visitor that evening."

"How long were you there for?"

"About four hours altogether."

"And why do you do it?"

"In this case, I like Danica's body and seeing her being pleasured by so many people."

"Why don't you visit her and pleasure her yourself?"

"She sneers at me whenever she sees me in the village, and I am old and fat and of no interest to her."

"I wouldn't have thought you were that old, Barry."

Knowles asked another question.

"How many times per week did you four go out stalking together?"

"We never went out together, but we each had our own pitches, our own places, and we always knew who was going to be entertaining visitors and who was going to be doing something interesting in the woods."

"Please tell us who you mean, Barry – who entertains and who goes into the woods?"

"I am not answering that question without a lawyer present."

"Are you scared that the other three have been killed by someone you have been watching?"

"No comment."

"Why would you say nothing – did one of them threaten you?"

"Yes, they did, Lord Avon if you must know."

"I can see why you'd want a lawyer having said that – his expensive lawyer would prosecute you for slander."

"I think I'd be OK, Inspector Knowles, I had the foresight to record his lordship's comment on my tape machine."

"And does he know that, Barry?"

"He does and he threatened me again, which was quite stupid because I recorded that comment too."

============

"Sometimes I think that everyone in Goat Parva is quite desperately dense," said Knowles as they walked away from the interview room, "why would Lord Avon threaten someone carrying a tape recorder – it's idiotic."

"Why would Lord Avon go into the woods and ride his stable boy on a regular basis anyway? It's almost as though he wants to be seen and admired for his athletic prowess – perhaps he's a frustrated bull rider from the American Wild West or he's never been allowed to take part in the Calgary Stampede?"

"And why does it have to be the stable boy that he rides? But then again his wife is probably drunk by lunch time."

"Do you think the riding ever turns sexual or that his lordship has ever tried to ride somebody else?"

"I wouldn't have thought there was ever any sex with the stable boy, but I do wonder why he wouldn't visit Danica as she's only next door – he could ride her I'm sure and in the comfort of her home too rather than in the woods with the lad."

"Speaking of Danica, should we let Janus go, so she can sneer at him whenever she meets him?"

"Let him go now, but go home with him and take his tape machine, as he called it, and find that threat from Lord Avon and keep it as evidence in our enquiry. Also, put two plain clothes constables on his case and watch Janus' house just in case there is someone after him we don't know about."

"Right, I will do that, sir, and where will you go?"

"I, Sergeant Barnes, am going to see Danica Baker-Clements and question her about her statement that she was normally watched by three people on Tuesdays – I believe, I think, those three are all dead now and I want to know how she knew there were three."

"You give yourself all the difficult jobs, don't you, sir?" said Barnes with a large hint of irony. "I get an old, sad, pervert and you get a young, femme fatale – where's the justice in that?"

"You're getting the more honest of the two, Barnesy, my lad, so you mustn't forget that."

"That will be a source of comfort for me as I have to listen to his detailed ramblings regarding his stalking exploits."

"When he does talk about his stalking exploits make sure you're listening because he might say something that's pertinent to our investigation – I haven't completely ruled him out being the murderer. And don't forget to get plain clothes on to him without his knowledge."

"What about the constable who was watching the PO box – could he be used?"

"No, he can stay where he is just in case Mr Janus is lying and there are more of them out there. The constable can stay there one more day and then perhaps take over one of the Janus observations."

"Presumably plain clothes should follow him if he leaves the house?"

"Barry is not to leave the house under any circumstances on his own – he must be accompanied even if he's going to photograph a hedge or a river."

"Did you want us to get the other DVDs in the PO box or leave them there for another day…?"

"…Just in case somebody else opens the box and decides to have a look around? Yes, we should leave them there for that extra day."

"Do you think someone else is in the stalking club, sir? It doesn't seem likely. Barry Janus seemed to think he was the only one left."

"One of the four might have shared his/her images with somebody else without telling Barry. After all, I am sure that the four of them never met each other at the same time."

"How strange – a club whose members never all meet at the same time."

"And now never will do – at least in this life."

===========

As Barnes escorted Barry Janus back to his house on the edge of Goat Parva, Colin Knowles prepared himself to meet Danica Baker-Clements again. He decided that he should write his questions down like Sergeant Barnes did, though for different reasons, of course. Was she spying on the people who were spying on her or was she getting some help from a friend? Why did she despise Barry Janus so much? Were there ever more than three people watching her at any one time?

Knowles looked in the mirror and convinced himself that the diet was definitely working. He slicked back his hair slightly and placed a mint in his mouth for that extra fresh breath. He even took his Land Rover through the carwash on the edge of Scoresby before heading out to Goat Parva. He turned right after St Timothy's church and headed down her drive. He couldn't help noticing that the lounge window where she paraded was easily viewable from around 80 yards of bushes on three sides.

Plenty of room for four or five stalkers to watch in almost splendid isolation, thought Knowles as he loosened his tie slightly before ringing her bell. He waited for around 20 seconds and then the door was unlocked. Danica stood before him in a loose-fitting knee length red skirt that shrieked sexiness.

"Hello, Inspector Knowles, how are you, do come inside?"

"Thank you, Mrs Baker-Clements."

"Do call me Danica. Now how can I help you this time?"

Knowles sat opposite her and couldn't help noticing an expanse of tanned thigh right in his line of vision. He tried to remember his questions.

"Last time we visited you indicated that you knew three people always watched you on Tuesday evenings, and I was wondering how you knew that and if you knew who those three people were?"

"Well, I was hoping that nice Sergeant Barnes would be returning to see me, so be sure to pass on my regards to him, Inspector. How do I know there were three people watching me on Tuesdays, well I speak to Poppy Avon sometimes and she told me that her brother Claude, I think that's his name, has a telescope and he watches me through that telescope, but he also spies on the people spying on me. Claude told Poppy that Clem Shapiro, Barry Janus, and Carol Herald usually watched me on Tuesdays. They watched on other days of the week too, but not on a regular basis. Your PC Davis also watched me, but not regularly, possibly because of his shift work. Apparently Carol used to bring a friend along with her on occasions, probably that ugly woman from the animal shelter in Madeley."

"So Claude Avon also watched you? How does that make you feel?"

"Well, one more doesn't make much difference, Inspector, but it's embarrassing someone that young should be a pervert; I don't know what I'd do if I met him or even had to talk to him, given that he's seen me in the nude."

"You could always close the curtains or watch the TV in a room at the back of the house, Danica. It's an easily solvable problem."

"Is that your way of saying that the lady doth protesteth too much? I just want to behave the way I want to in my own house – is that not my right?"

"Absolutely, but you can't complain if that behaviour causes people to watch you from the bushes – you could call the police and ask them to remove the observers from your property."

"They're not on my property though; they're on public land either in Hen's Wood or on Doggett's Field."

"Or they are by the time the police get here."

"If you turned off the sirens then perhaps they wouldn't move until it was too late."

"Well, when you ring up to complain then ask the duty sergeant to tell the boys in blue to switch off the sirens in order to make sure that the watchers aren't forewarned."

"Thank you for the information, Inspector – I wonder who will replace Carol and Clem on Tuesday, now they are no longer alive? That horrid Barry Janus will no doubt be there watching me."

"Actually, Danica you were being watched by four people on Tuesday, including Barry, but don't worry he won't be watching you again – we had him in for questioning and he will be accompanied everywhere by an officer. He told us that you sneer at him when you see him in the street."

"Of course I do, he stares at my breasts and inner thighs and winks at me."

"So you won't have an audience to worry about on Tuesday, Danica."

"Other than Claude Avon of course."

"Other than dear Claude and I think he may have stopped watching you by then too."

"Why do you say that, Inspector Knowles?"

"It's just a feeling I have, Danica, just a feeling."

Knowles stood up and was escorted to the door by Danica.

"Was this just a visit for police business or was there anything else I could help you with today, Inspector?"

"I am still on duty, thank you. I have a couple of other people to see now."

"I will just have to have a shower on my own then, Inspector. Close the door behind you if you will. Don't forget to mention me to Sergeant Barnes."

Danica Baker-Clements walked towards the stairs and unhooked her dress so that it fell to the floor revealing her red, lace underwear.

Knowles had some difficulty getting his erection through the door. He drove his vehicle to the top of her drive and then switched the ignition off. He sat in his Land Rover taking a mental cold shower for a few minutes while his heart calmed down. His phone rang.

"'Allo, Knowles here, hello, Barnesy…So our Barry is tucked up in bed, and plain clothes is watching…yes that's good…no she was very forward with me and so tempting, but she's a suspect still as her evidence doesn't match what other people have told me. Right see you at the station tomorrow morning...yes, unless our Bingo dog finds another body of course."

Knowles was about to start the ignition when he saw the postman riding his bike along the road. He veered past Knowles without seeing him, so intent was he on the prize. Knowles saw the smile on the cyclist's face and muttered "Lucky bastard" under his breath. When the investigation was over, perhaps he could be less professional...

Chapter 7

WPC Linda Smythe stationed herself outside The Cottage in Goat Parva and waited for someone to go for a walk. Her strict instructions were to not allow the retriever or the owner out of her sight and to ensure that she stayed by any bodies that the dog found during his morning walk so that no contamination of the crime scene could take place. Linda had been asked to wear plain clothes, so that no one would think that Adelaide Hills was under police escort.

Linda noticed the village was beginning to wake up – a young man with a gym bag came out of the woods and went into a house on the other side of the road. He was soon followed by a younger man with a long lens and a tripod who headed towards her, but on the other side of the road. An older lady carrying a basket headed towards Linda, but disappeared into a driveway; she was closely followed by a middle-aged man who headed into the shop. Finally another figure, a younger girl this time, came out of the woods and ran over to the pub car park. She got into a red, expensive car and zoomed away from Linda heading south along the Leicester Road.

At 7:30am the front door of The Cottage opened and a barking retriever emerged closely followed by his owner. Adelaide Hills looked at Linda with some distaste.

"Who are you?"

"I am WPC Linda Smythe, Mrs Hills, and I am to accompany you and your hound on your morning walk."

"He's not a hound – he's a purebred retriever I will have you know – so Inspector Knowles has carried through his threat to have me escorted on the morning walk?"

"It's not so much you, Mrs Hills, it's Bongo that he's concerned about and his uncanny ability to find dead bodies."

"*Bingo* is a retriever and he retrieves items because that's his instinct."

"There's another word for those items and that is 'evidence', Mrs Hills. It also seems as though someone interferes with the bodies after you have left them and before the police arrive, so I will wait by the body until my colleagues arrive."

"You are really expecting another body to be found, aren't you?"

"Inspector Knowles isn't taking any chances – he reckons the odds of us finding a body today are only 30-70, but we have to cover every eventuality."

"Of course we do – I am sure Bingo will do his best to confound those odds, but I am not putting any money on it."

"Where will we walk today?"

"Well, WPC Smythe, I am sure you are aware that there are a number of crime scenes here in Goat Parva, so we will have to head into Culpepper's Woods, but avoid the leafy glade and keep to the hedge by the road for the first two hundred yards. We can head towards Madeley Waterless."

WPC Linda Smythe nodded and allowed her two wards to walk ten yards ahead of her. They turned left through the gate into the woods and then turned right to keep close to the hedge. This must be where the young man with the bag and the younger man with the tripod came from. And the young woman who jumped into the car. It was strange that there were no footprints in the wet ground of people coming towards them – where had those people come from then? They must have walked across the crime scene. Linda Smythe made a note to check when they returned at the end of their walk. She heard a fox cry in the distance as the rain began to fall and neutralise the odours of the woods.

Suddenly Bingo barked and ran off into the undergrowth with his tail wagging vigorously. Mrs Hills turned around and shouted.

"He's found something I just know it – I wonder who it will be this time."

Linda Smythe walked over to Mrs Hills and waited to see what Bingo would bring. They didn't have to wait very long – he came bounding back carrying something in his mouth.

"Bingo please drop the object on to the ground – drop it now, Bingo."

Bingo dropped the object on the ground and Mrs Hills let out a cry.

"That's my mobile phone – where did you find this, Bingo, where did this come from?"

"When did you lose it?" asked WPC Smythe.

"About three days ago, at home, I thought Bingo had stolen it – what's it doing out here?"

"Could he have buried it in the woods without you knowing it?"

"No – he never comes out on his own – even if he did, why would he come this far? It's a long way to bury something – I have a large back garden too."

"Could you prompt him to show us where he found the phone?"

"I can try. Bingo, here's your toy – fetch, Bingo."

Mrs Hills had taken the precaution of placing Bingo on a lead before allowing him to show them where the phone had been found. Bingo led Mrs Hills into the undergrowth and stopped on a flat patch of ground. He barked and dropped the phone.

"Here, Bingo, did you find the phone here?"

"Someone has been lying down here – you can tell because the plants have been flattened by a large weight – I wonder if the body has been removed by someone else or whether the person was stalking a victim."

"Another person got to the body before Bingo – well that's quite a relief – Bingo, you're losing your touch."

"Mrs Hills, can I have the phone please – thank you – now can you please go home and report the find to the police as you have done with the others? I will wait here to see if anyone comes back here. Don't mention me to anyone you see."

"I will go home and I won't tell – I know Sergeant Barnes' number off by heart now."

Linda Smythe nodded and watched as Mrs Hills headed

back to the main road. The WPC then found a spot where she could observe the place where the phone was found without being seen. She took out her phone with its camera and waited.

After 10 minutes the woman whom Linda had seen earlier carrying a basket came into her line of vision. The woman looked around on the ground for a few minutes in some desperation and then shouted out "Where's it gone – it must be here somewhere?"

Suddenly the woman heard something and decided to hide behind a tree near to WPC Smythe. A few seconds later Sergeant Barnes arrived with a uniformed constable. Barnes looked around on the ground and then produced a roll of tape and cordoned off the area. Lynda Smythe wanted to shout out to Barnes, but didn't want to betray her position to the woman who was hiding behind a nearby tree. Suddenly Smythe remembered her phone. She rang Barnes' number and spoke in a low voice when he answered.

"Sergeant Barnes – it's WPC Smythe here…"

"Speak up, Lynda – I can hardly hear you."

"I can't speak up, I am behind a tree and I can see you in the glade."

"What?"

"I'm behind a tree and I can see you."

"Well, come out and talk to me."

"I can't there's someone else hiding behind another tree close by. She's a suspect."

"A suspect behind a tree – which tree?"

"The oak tree."

"I'm not very good with trees – which tree is that?"

"Turn around through 180 degrees."

Barnes turned around.

"It's the third one to your right, but don't look at it – I am behind the next tree but one to the right of the oak."

Barnes looked up in to the canopy of the wood and turned around again.

"Lynda, I will ask the constable to leave and then I will also leave, but I will go and hide behind a tree."

"Which tree will you hide behind?"

"There's a tree with a small boulder in front of it..."

"The ash?"

"Perhaps, yes – I will wait there until our suspect comes into the open."

"Right – that sounds like a plan – what happens if the suspect doesn't come out into the open?"

"We'll give it 20 minutes and then if there's nothing happening phone me back."

"OK – I will do that."

Lynda rang off and watched as Barnes very ostentatiously and woodenly motioned the constable to vacate the scene – he wasn't going to win many acting awards, she thought. Barnes then surveyed the scene with his hand over his eyes and hurried away towards the road. After about 100 yards he stopped and doubled back keeping low to the ground before coming to a halt behind the ash tree. He was in position.

For about 15 minutes nobody moved and then the woman suspect broke her cover and walked over to the cordoned off area. She got down on her knees and started to search the ground very keenly.

Smythe's phone vibrated – it was Barnes.

"Is that her?"

"Yes, that's the one – the only one I know about anyway – there are a few trees around, so perhaps there might be others."

Barnes ignored the sarcasm. "That's Carly Waferr – let's see what she does and we won't interfere for now."

"Right, oh, I have another call coming – it's Inspector Knowles, I'd better take it...Hello, Inspector..I am whispering because I am hiding behind a tree."

As Smythe listened to Inspector Knowles she watched Carly Waferr scrabbling around in the dirt.

"I am hiding because a suspect is searching the ground in the woods looking for something...no the dog didn't find a body this morning...yes, you would have won your bet, but Bingo did find a phone that Mrs Hills had lost a few days ago. Sergeant Barnes? He's hiding behind a tree...no a different tree, an ash tree, my tree is a chestnut tree...yes under the spreading chestnut tree…and he believes the suspect is Carly Waferr. She had been hiding behind an oak tree. Yes, lots of different trees species to hide behind."

Carly Waferr stood up and hurled abuse at Mother Nature and her thieves before bursting into tears and wandering off into the deeper woods, away from both Barnes and Smythe.

"Should I arrest Carly Waferr, Inspector Knowles, she's leaving the scene of a possible crime?…No, right I will let her go then. Thanks, Inspector, anyway I should go as Barnes is trying to contact me…hello, Sergeant, no we should let her go…Inspector Knowles said so. Anyway, I think we can stop whispering now as she's out of sight. Right, oh hold on what was that?"

A twig had snapped and Smythe saw a hooded figure running towards the edge of the woods near the Leicester Road. She quickly took a picture with her camera.

"Who was that?" said Barnes, "and how long have they been hiding for?"

"I am not sure, but they came from behind that horse chestnut tree over there."

"Why are you so good at identifying trees?" asked Barnes.

"It's from my I-spy book of trees and from biology class at school," said Smythe, as she headed to the hiding place of the hooded person.

"You remember details very well," replied Barnes. "This is the place isn't it?"

"It is and it looks like whoever it was had been kneeling down for a while – oh look, there's a black thread." Smythe found an evidence bag and placed the thread inside and handed the bag over to Barnes.

"There you are, Sergeant, some evidence for you."

"Thank you, Constable – oh, what was that?"

Both of them heard a number of twigs snapping.

"Don't tell me there's yet another stalker around here," said Barnes, but then he heard the familiar wheezing of a cigarette-smoking Inspector.

Knowles appeared in the glade and waved to them.

"Hello, Inspector, guess what happened after you stopping talking to the Constable here?"

"Well, let me guess, Sergeant Barnes – this is Goat Parva, so I would imagine that there was another stalker that none of you were aware of until they broke cover. And because this is deciduous woodland I would also guess that they were concealed behind a different species of tree from you, Smythe, and that Waferr woman."

"That's impressive, sir, especially about the trees."

"Not really, Smythe already gave me a detailed list of the hiding places of the various protagonists and you are standing by a Horse Chestnut tree, so it was worth a try. Any idea who the stalker was?"

"Fit looking and wore a dark-coloured hoodie that was made of whatever material this is," replied Smythe pointing at the evidence bag in Barnes' hand. "And I have a picture on my phone which I can hand over to Forensics." She handed the phone to Knowles who scowled.

"Not exactly conclusive, but it might be useful, good work, Constable." He handed the phone back. "And which way did they head?"

"The opposite way to Carly Waferr, towards Leicester Road, whereas Waferr headed towards Madeley Waterless."

"Why would Waferr head away from her home?" wondered Barnes.

Knowles thought for a minute before he said, "My guess is she had to go and tell someone the mobile phone that Waferr stole has been returned to its rightful owner – but who would be interested in knowing that and why would Waferr have taken it in the first place?"

"Because whoever it is knows that Adelaide Hills has a dog that interferes with people's stalking activities and that finds objects, which might incriminate people under certain circumstances. If you steal her phone she can't phone us straightaway giving people time to leave the scene after she's gone home to report to the police."

"That's a good thought, Barnesy, but does this mean that Carly Waferr is an accomplice to three murders or is she unwittingly helping this other person or persons unknown?"

"It's possible that they don't want to have Adelaide Hills discover something in the near future – it doesn't have to be related to the murders, but to some forthcoming illegal activity – perhaps the animal protesters are planning to break into some research institute nearby like the one down by the river. Adelaide Hills might be walking Bingo down there and report the crime."

"That farm's about a mile away and I don't think Mrs Hills walks that far. However, animal protesters might have something to do with it as those girls at the animal sanctuary at Madeley Waterless are supposedly quite militant and Carly Waferr was heading that way. Here's what we will do, Sergeant Barnes – get a plain clothes man to Madeley Waterless and ask him to watch out for people leaving the animal shelter."

"I will do that right now, Inspector," said Barnes and headed off towards his vehicle.

"WPC Smythe," said Knowles, "when you arrived outside Mrs Hills' house, what activity did you see in the village – anything unusual that you can remember?"

Linda Smythe told the inspector about the young man with a gym bag, another younger man with a long lens and a tripod, the woman carrying a basket, who she now knew to be Carly Waferr, the middle-aged man who headed into the shop, and finally the younger girl who ran over to the pub car park and roared off in an expensive, red car.

"Five people – we know one was definitely Carly Waferr, the young man with the gym bag was Mr Greggs and the one with the tripod was Claude Avon, whose sister was the one heading to the red car – her name is Poppy. Which only leaves the man heading into the shop. The shop wouldn't be open at that time, so I wonder if it was the owner, Tom Jargoy? Let's head there now and see if we can find him. Then we can head back to the station afterwards."

The two police headed away from the glade watched all the way by the stalker who had hidden behind a wall. The stalker smiled as they disappeared from view and then hurried away to Madeley Waterless – Carly Waferr would have to be told not to use the animal shelter by the front entrance.

===========

Smythe looked through the front window and couldn't see anyone at first until a woman with an expensive cardigan came into the shop, via an inside door, and started to look at her.

"Sir, I think it might be best if I go inside and have a browse around – the owner's looking at me suspiciously."

"That's fine, Constable, carry on - just don't buy anything too expensive to put on your expenses."

Linda Smythe went inside and thought she should buy some bran flakes for her breakfast as she hadn't eaten yet – 7am was a bit early for her to wake up let alone be on duty. She was approached by Brenda Jargoy.

"Didn't I see you hanging around outside Adelaide Hills' house earlier this morning?"

"You would have done yes, I accompanied her on the morning walk with her dog."

"Why did you do that – just in case Bingo found another body?"

"That was one of the reasons yes and there were others too."

"So you are the police?"

"Yes, I am although I am working undercover. When I was outside this morning I noticed that a man came out of the woods and headed towards the shop – any idea who that might have been?"

"We weren't open at that time, so I am not sure who it was."

"Well the man didn't come away from the shop again, so I got the impression he went inside – when we walked past there was nobody outside so he must have entered the shop."

Brenda Jargoy wasn't sure what to say as she knew that the constable was referring to her husband, Tom Jargoy, but she hadn't been aware that he'd ventured out so early. She was wondering where he'd gone.

"Was there anyone else around this morning who might be able to help you with your enquiries?"

"There were a number of other people around yes, but I haven't spoken to them yet."

"Right, well if I hear anything in the shop I will let you know."

"Thank you – I am WPC Linda Smythe and you are?"

"Brenda Jargoy – pleased to meet you." She extended a limp, damp hand to the WPC who held it for a second and then let go.

"Mrs Jargoy?"

"Yes."

"Is Mr Jargoy around – perhaps he might have seen something?"

"Tom is out at the moment working on a job; he's a handyman – he didn't mention seeing anyone, but I will be sure to ask him who the man you saw might be."

"Please do let me know what he says, Mrs Jargoy. Here's my card and that's my direct line." WPC Smythe smiled inwardly as she left the shop – Mrs Jargoy hadn't known that Mr Jargoy had been in the woods that morning, so what had he been up to and with whom?

Knowles was lurking outside and Barnes was talking on his phone to the plain clothes officer at the animal shelter in Madeley Waterless. Smythe told Knowles about her conversation.

"I'd bet my mortgage, or Barnesy's mortgage at least, that it was Tom Jargoy you saw this morning and that he'd been seeing Carly Waferr – they were romantically involved on the ground in the woods and she lost her newly acquired phone in the action, which is how everyone's friend, Bingo the hound, found it."

"That Waferr woman has to be at least sixty – who'd want to have her?"

"She's not aged well, WPC Smythe. Too many magic mushrooms and elderberry wine."

"I thought mushrooms were supposed to be good for you and an excellent source of selenium?"

"Well look at Carly Waferr and see for yourself whether that's true – maybe the elderberries are to blame."

Barnes chimed in. "She drinks lots of elderberry wine I

think, so perhaps that's the reason – it's the alcohol content of her diet that's the problem."

"Without finding out her entire diet we can't be sure why she's apparently aged so badly – perhaps she eats lots of bread, wheat-based bread rather than rye," opined Smythe.

"Does that age you?" asked Knowles in a concerned manner – he ate lots of wheat-based food.

"Oh yes, Inspector, some of the newest research on the Internet does indicate that's true."

"That's bad news for me – I eat boxes of Weetabix and Shredded Wheat each week – well, the contents of the boxes; I will have to re-evaluate my diet." Knowles patted his stomach as if to emphasise the point.

"Something else we will have to re-evaluate is whether Carly Waferr was going to the animal shelter this morning – plain clothes say that she hasn't been seen there so far."

"That bastard stalker must have intercepted her before she got near the place, which means that the stalker must be connected with the shelter in some way."

"Either that or the stalker knows Carly Waferr and whatever it is she's been up to."

"Should we speak to Waferr, sir?" asked WPC Smythe.

"We most definitely should," said Knowles, "but first I think Barnesy and I will visit Lord Avon again and ask him what Claude and Poppy were doing this morning in the woods around 7am. Meanwhile, WPC Smythe, please take your phone and evidence bag back to the station to Forensics; then have some breakfast – without any wheat of course – and then drive back here and keep an eye on Waferr's house and see if she comes back."

"And if and when she returns I will phone you straightaway."

"Great – we will be over as soon as possible – if she leaves again follow her and let me know."

"Understood, sir, see you later."

============

A few minutes later, Knowles pulled the rope that rang the bell in the servants' quarters at Langstroth Hall.

After around two minutes the large wooden door lurched open and the butler stood there with a stern countenance.

"Gentlemen, how can I help you?"

"That was a lot longer than last time – standards are slipping - I am Detective Inspector Knowles and this is Detective Sergeant Barnes – we'd like to speak to Claude and Poppy Avon and we don't have an appointment, just in case you were going to ask."

"Please wait in the atrium here if you will."

As he spoke the butler gestured to the area just inside the door. He then walked stiffly down the corridor and entered the door at the far end. After a minute he returned.

"I'm afraid that his lordship is indisposed now, but Master Claude, Miss Poppy, and her ladyship will see you in the summerhouse in 4 minutes. Turn right outside the front door and head along the path and you will come to the summerhouse."

"Thank you, we will vacate the premises straightaway," Knowles said through pursed lips and opened the front door.

After the front door had been closed behind them Barnes let out a laugh.

"Indisposed – what does that mean? He's recovering from his latest escapade in the woods with the stable boy? Or is he tired from having sex with someone other than his wife?"

"Both, from what I have heard," grunted Knowles, "now let's make sure we step on these stepping stones and don't touch the grass."

Barnes and Knowles found the three Avons already ensconced in the summerhouse and Lady Avon had a drink in her hand, a drink that almost certainly wasn't her first of the day as she almost toasted the police when they stepped inside the large glass and white wood structure.

"Detectives – it's good to see you again, how can we help you this time? Do sit down on one of the foot rests."

"Thank you," grinned Knowles, "we'll stand for now. Lady Avon – our plain clothes constable saw both Claude and Poppy coming out of Culpepper's Woods this morning around 7am, so I would like to know what they were doing in the woods this morning."

Claude and Poppy looked at each other with obvious impatience. Poppy spoke first.

"Well, firstly, there's no reason why I shouldn't be in those woods at that time, but as you asked I will tell you out of the goodness of my own heart. I went in there for a meditative walk. I am trying to have more Buddhism in my life and that wood is the most peaceful place in the village although this morning it was relatively noisy as someone was having sex in one of the leafy glades, but I removed that from my mind and concentrated on my breathing and on the wind blowing in my face."

"How do you know someone was having sex?" asked Barnes.

"Put your tongue away, Detective," said Lady Avon with a slight leer.

"I could tell from the noises that the couple were making."

"And who were the couple involved?" asked Knowles, with a good idea of the answer.

"Yah - one was Carly Waferr and I am not sure who the other person was," interrupted Claude. "I saw her patting down her skirts when I was coming out of the woods after taking some pictures of the trees in the early morning light."

"And did either of you see anyone creeping around wearing a hoodie and gloves in the woods?"

"No, but I did think I was being watched at one point, but I usually feel that at some point in those woods – they can be creepy on occasions," said Claude.

"I was concentrating on my breathing so I wasn't aware of the presence of anyone else, other than the noises I told you about already," replied Poppy.

"You seemed to leave the woods in a bit of a hurry."

"Well, my meditation worked really well and I lost track of time and then I realised I was late to meet a friend and so I was in a hurry."

"And you, Claude – your pictures of the trees how did they turn out?"

"Not that bad actually, the only problem is getting the tripod straight and I am just glad I have a spirit level to make sure."

"Did you see Mr Greggs the banker when you were in the woods, Claude?"

"I might have – he tends to stand in the same spot and do his tai-chi so he almost blends into the background as it were; you don't always notice the familiar of course."

"That's very true," mused Knowles, "and very profound too, Claude because there was something missing this morning and I am not sure what it was."

"What on earth do you mean, man?" screeched Lady Avon.

"I mean that there was something not quite right this morning, something missing, and I don't just mean there was no body discovered this morning."

"There was no-one else taking pictures in the woods this morning; Barry Janus wasn't around," said Claude, "he's normally in the woods or over by the river, but I didn't see him at all. Did you see him, Popps?"

Poppy Avon shook her head and then added, "Was the postman around this morning, I don't remember seeing him either?"

"The postman was around, slightly later than normal at 9am, I seem to remember," said Lady Avon, "he came here and made a delivery at that time."

"Barry Janus wasn't around this morning was he? I wonder where Barry is?" said Knowles, without fully knowing the answer. Janus should be under surveillance but resources were stretched due to the Waferr woman and he hoped that Janus hadn't escaped detection.

"Claude – do you and Barry ever compare photographic images?" enquired Barnes.

"My son would never consort with that awful man," harrumphed Lady Avon and rose unsteadily to get another drink from the decanter.

"He's not awful. He did show me some wonderful pictures of the river on his camera a few weeks ago," replied Claude sniffily.

Lady Avon slammed the decanter down onto the table and glared at Claude – Poppy looked at her with a mixture of embarrassment and sadness.

"Well, I've spoken to Barry too and he's perfectly pleasant – I do wonder what he's taking pictures of sometimes though as he's somewhat furtive."

"He's one of those stalkers," said Lady Avon sitting down with a great deal of care, "he used to spend a lot of time with the three people who were murdered. I have seen them talking outside Danica Baker-Clements' place sometimes."

"And where were you at the time, Lady Avon?" queried Barnes.

"Watching from my bedroom window if you must know, through a telescope. And no, I didn't see anything the night that the pig person Clement Shapiro was killed before you ask."

"I was going to ask, so how often did you see them together?"

"Actually I never did make a note in my diary, Inspector, so I will have to rely on my memory – perhaps once a week? I was never a voyeur myself you see, but once one sees people creeping around near one's property then one becomes more protective and one watches more and more."

"I understand one would, Lady Avon – did you ever see anything strange or were there ever any different people from normal?"

"I can't really think of anyone – oh wait a minute, now there was someone different there a couple of weeks ago with Carol Herald. Whoever it was wore an overall and I thought I recognised her, but I can't for the life of me remember…do you have a card, Inspector with your direct line so I can phone you?"

Knowles rummaged in his jacket and came up with a card which he handed to Lady Avon, who graciously accepted it.

"Thank you, Inspector, is there anything else we can help you with?"

"Well, yes, you said you thought you recognised her, how sure are you that it was a her, especially as the person was wearing an overall?"

"The shape, Inspector, especially the curvier parts of the body."

"Just so long as you're sure, that's the most important thing," continued Knowles. "Now I would like to ask one question to Poppy."

Poppy Avon looked startled.

Knowles continued, "Poppy, according to two eye witnesses, you had an exchange, a heated exchange with Carol Herald and threatened her after she chided you for maltreating your toy dog; dying it green, not feeding it, blaming the shelter for giving you an unhealthy dog – that sort of thing. Any comments, Poppy?"

"It was about three months ago, when Mungo, that's my boyfriend of the time, was being a total dick to me and I rather took it out on Montague – my behaviour towards him was just a cry for help in a cynical and uninterested world."

"You dyed Montague green though?"

"It was a vegetable dye and didn't harm him; he enjoyed being green until he was run over by the gardener driving the lawnmower."

There was a very awkward silence.

"Poppy, did you ever follow through on your threat towards Carol Herald?"

"I didn't, Inspector, I am not a violent person by nature and I would not physically hurt another human being or animal. I am trying to make it part of my Buddhist training."

"Well, if that's all then do please see yourselves out," said Lady Avon and headed over towards the drinks tray.

"We will – thank you everyone, that's been most useful," said Knowles and he led Barnes out of the summerhouse.

Once they were by the front door Barnes let out a large sigh of relief.

"Thank God we're out of the goldfish bowl. Sit on the footrests indeed! Who the hell does she think she is?"

"The Lady of the Manor," said Knowles, "but I think we might have a breakthrough thanks to her, especially if she can remember who the extra person was that she saw."

"Well, sir, in my opinion, I doubt she will remember saying that let alone remember the actual person she was referring to. She must have been drunk when we arrived. And she has a very low opinion of Barry Janus for some reason and yet he does exactly what Claude does in terms of snooping around."

"I think Lady Avon doesn't want Claude to get any ideas from Barry – can you check with plain clothes and make sure he's still at home and hasn't absconded? Thanks Barnesy. I will phone WPC Smythe and see where she is."

"Constable – yes, it's Knowles – you aren't hiding behind a tree this time then? Right…you've just arrived and she's not around…blend into the background, because she will come back and then we shall pounce on her. Literally pounce as if from behind a tree…she will be charged with theft and attempting to pervert the course of justice at the very least…I will let you go…Sergeant Barnes looks worried."

"Sergeant Barnes is worried – plain clothes stayed outside the Janus residence and then one of them was called to Madeley Waterless to look out for Carly Waferr, so the other one had two entrances to look after and it seems like Janus has gone out the back door whilst plain clothes was at the front."

"And this was about an hour ago? Right get plain clothes to call for two constables and get them to look in Hen's Wood and on the river bank for Janus – also disable his dung-coloured vehicle so he can't leave. Make sure someone is still looking at the PO box in the Post Office just in case he goes there again."

"Consider it done," said Barnes and started to make his calls.

Knowles' phone rang – it was WPC Smythe.

"Sir, that man I saw this morning – he's just come back again and disappeared into the shop as he did earlier – he was running and looked a bit anxious."

"From which direction did he come?"

"He came along Sharrock Lane from the river – actually sir you should come right over here because I think I have just seen someone come into Carly Waferr's garden from the woods."

"Where are you?"

"I am behind the oak tree in the Badger and Ferret car park."

"Going for the full set of trees today, Constable, that's good – OK Barnes and I will walk down Leicester Road and turn down Sharrock Lane- I will double back and join you. See you in a minute."

Knowles joined Barnes and motioned to him to walk down the Langstroth House drive to the main road. When Barnes had finished on the phone, Knowles told him what WPC Smythe had seen and what had been arranged. Barnes should walk down Sharrock Lane to the river and turn north towards Hen's Wood keeping a look out for Barry Janus.

"Barnesy, when you leave me phone plain clothes at Madeley and ask them kindly to return to the Janus residence just in case our Barry has doubled back on himself. They should stay there until they hear otherwise."

"Understood, sir. Will you be visiting Carly Waferr, if it is her?"

"I will be doing, though at first I will wait to see if Tom Jargoy visits her again."

"Again?"

"They had an early morning assignation this morning, Sergeant. I wonder why he was running back from the river a few minutes ago? Anyway, here's the main road let's amble down the footpath and completely ignore anything on our left hand side until we reach Sharrock."

As he walked down the road Knowles stared at the oak tree in the pub car park but couldn't for the life of him see WPC Smythe – she was good - he wasn't sure he would fit behind the tree and looked at his stomach, wishing it would reduce in size.

"How's the diet, sir, losing any weight?"

"No, not yet, but from what Smythe was saying, I am probably eating far too much wheat in my diet – I need to do more exercise as well where my heart rate increases to above 120 beats per minute."

"Take it gradually, sir and wear a heart monitor so you can see the rate and reduce the intensity if it increases too quickly."

"Yes, good advice, Sergeant. Anyway, we should cross and see what happens next. Do let me know if you find our friend Barry."

"You will be the first to know, sir," smiled Barnes as he headed off to the river. Knowles watched him make the call to the plain clothes at Madeley and then headed into the pub car park to find WPC Smythe. The oak tree was on a low mound and Smythe had hollowed out one small area between the roots so that she could see Leicester Road heading northwards and also Carly Waferr's garden. She had parked her car so that she couldn't be seen from Sharrock Lane. Knowles crouched down to speak to Smythe.

"Will I be OK here; will they see me from over there?"

"Sit on this mat by the wheel arch and you will be fine, sir."

Knowles took off his jacket and sat on the mat.

"What have you seen recently?"

"Not a great deal – two men walking innocently down Leicester Road without a care in the world and trying not to look to their left."

"You saw us? I didn't see you – you should run a course – how to hide behind different species of tree, telegraph poles, and hedges."

"We should think about that, sir. Anyway, I am sure that I saw someone enter Carly Waferr's garden from the woods, so should we go and investigate to see if she's there?"

"I think we should wait to see whether Tom Jargoy puts in an appearance – let's wait 15 minutes and see."

============

As Knowles concealed himself behind a tree, Barnes headed towards the river and gave the instructions to the plain clothes officer at Madeley Waterless. He then turned north towards the woods and started looking for Barry Janus. He was sure that Janus was either hiding from the police or had been attacked and so might be in plain sight. As he headed into the woods he saw two police constables in the distance looking around on the ground. The plain clothes officer was also dragging dead branches away from possible hiding places. Barnes looked around to see if he could discern any broken branches or trodden down foliage that would indicate someone had recently come in this direction but there was nothing definite.

Suddenly there was a shout from the plain clothes officer; Barnes made his way towards the man as did the two uniforms. He was holding aloft a blue bag as big as a child's satchel, whose strap was broken.

"Here you are, sir," said the plain clothes officer, "I found this thrown into that tree stump."

"Thanks, John," said Barnes putting on a pair of plastic gloves. "Let's see what we can find."

Barnes opened the bag quite carefully and peered inside – he saw a few clothes, mainly underwear, and a toilet bag containing a toothbrush, razor, and toothpaste.

"I am guessing this was Janus' bag – I would also guess that he didn't throw this in the tree stump, so let's put this in an evidence bag and find the man himself. He has been attacked, but not by the murderer of the three others as that person would have taken this bag with them."

Barnes put the whole bag into a large, plastic bag and sealed it tight.

"Janus' house is in that direction so let's fan out four abreast and walk in that direction until we see something that's not quite right."

After about 10 yards one of the uniformed officers spotted a bloodstain on a tree. Barnes marked the tree with a ribbon and the four continued until another bloodstain was seen on a large fern.

"He seems to be heading towards the church," said Barnes, "presumably because it's the only place where he knew he would be able to find someone."

There was more blood on the stile heading into the churchyard and when Barnes climbed over it, he saw Barry Janus lying against a grave. He had a large head wound, but was still breathing. Barnes called for the ambulance and was surprised to hear that one had already been called by the Reverend Strong.

"When was this," said Barnes, "are you sure it was St Timothy's in Goat Parva?"

"Absolutely," said the dispatcher, "we thought it was a crank call at first, body in a churchyard needs an ambulance – usually happens after the pubs have closed, but this was a bit early even for a serious alcoholic and we sent it off."

"Right, thank you – so the next question is – where is Reverend Strong?"

=============

Meanwhile, behind the tree in the pub car park, the 15 minutes had passed by quite slowly – Knowles was thinking about having a pint of best bitter but knew that he shouldn't because he was on duty and because he was on a diet – he wasn't sure which one of those reasons was the more important – so he contented himself with looking over at the trees swaying in the breeze in Culpepper's Woods.

At one point a red Ferrari drove by and Knowles briefly saw the three Avons, minus Lord Avon, as they passed. Just afterwards Mrs Jargoy came out of the shop and headed over to Langstroth Hall.

"Well, WPC Lynda Smythe, I think it is time to head over to the Waferr residence and see if she's there; would you like to go round the back and trip her up if she tries to escape?"

"You think she'll try and do one, sir? I would guess she will take an age to answer the door and then claim to have been asleep."

"You may well be right, but I am not so sure she's that cool under pressure; we shall see."

Knowles and Smythe walked over the road; Smythe sidled up Carly Waferr's garden path and stood by the back door, whereas Knowles went around the front. He knocked three times and waited; there was no reply and no sound from inside the house. He knocked three more times and peered through the windows; suddenly the bolts were withdrawn on the front door and Carly Waferr opened it quite slowly.

"Hello, who's there, what do you want?"

"Hello, Carly – it's Detective Inspector Knowles here, can I ask you a few questions? Inside."

"I suppose so, but I've only just woken up, so I might not be too coherent."

Knowles smiled. "I will just go and get my colleague," he said and walked round the house and beckoned Smythe to follow him inside.

"She has just woken up – you were right – so I wonder if she walks in her sleep?"

"We should ask her."

When Knowles and WPC Smythe were both in Carly Waferr's sitting room, Carly offered them a cup of coffee; she was making one anyway as she needed to feel more alert. They both declined.

Once Carly Waferr had made her coffee, she came and sat in her favourite brown armchair and looked up at the two officers who were both standing.

"How can I help you this time, Inspector?"

"What have you been doing this morning, Carly – have you been up to much?"

"Nothing out of the ordinary, Inspector, just collecting some mushrooms in Hen's Wood and then coming back here and falling asleep, which is why I need this you see." She gestured to the coffee.

"Do you sleepwalk, Carly?"

"What? Of course I don't – I'd know wouldn't I? I'd wake up in a different place from where I fell asleep."

Knowles shook his head quite vigorously.

"That's actually the wrong answer, Carly, because you do sleep walk – it's the only possible explanation given that you say you were asleep and the WPC here states categorically she saw you come through your garden gate from Culpepper's Woods."

"That's amazing because I had no idea that I walked in my sleep; you learn something every single day – thank you."

"And were you asleep earlier when the WPC here and my sergeant saw you in Culpepper's Woods looking for a mobile phone that you'd dropped on the floor during your sex session with Tom Jargoy? You even went and hid behind a chestnut tree when you heard the sergeant arriving."

"Oak tree, sir, it was oak."

"Right, of course, oak it was."

"I deny that completely – why would I have sex when I was asleep? I am sure I would have remembered that."

"Do you also deny heading towards Madeley Waterless when it became clear you couldn't find the phone that had by that time been restored to its rightful owner – the person you stole it from, Mrs Adelaide Hills?"

"I do deny that, Inspector Knowles – I must have been asleep to wander off to Madeley Waterless when I live here – that shows I was asleep; it's completely the wrong direction."

Carly drank her coffee with a triumphant flourish; even she'd been impressed by her answer.

"Does Tom Jargoy know you were asleep this morning when you two were going at it in the woods?"

"I don't remember any such event this morning in the woods, Inspector Knowles."

"I think Tom will be disappointed to hear you say that – I will let him know that's how it was for you."

"Did he rape you, Carly?" asked WPC Smythe, "because if he did then you should press charges against him."

"I don't know – I was asleep I told you."

"We should take you down to the station, Carly, and take a urine test to see if he used Rohypnol on you."

"Did he make you drink anything?"

"I was asleep."

"You need a test, Carly, we should find out what made you so forgetful – I wonder how he made you drink that drug when you were asleep; it's quite a difficult thing to do I would have thought."

Knowles' phone rang…it was Barnes.

"He's been found where…but then the Reverend Strong disappeared…has he said anything…yes, I think he will be my next port of call as he's been administering Rohypnol to Carly Waferr…this morning…no when you saw her this morning she was sleep walking…yes she was…that's why she didn't find the phone…yes, makes sense now doesn't it?

Go with Janus to the hospital and let me know if he says anything. Thanks, Barnesy."

"What's happened to Barry Janus?" asked Carly.

"Nothing that you should be concerned with, Carly, after all you were asleep this morning – please go with WPC Smythe to the station at Scoresby and be prepared to take a urine test."

"I might have woken up and gone back to sleep again – you never know."

"Carly Waferr – where are your keys? Let's lock your house and take you to the station."

Carly Waferr stood up and walked into the kitchen, picked up her keys from next to the mushroom basket, and put on her coat. She was ready. Knowles motioned to her to give him the keys as he didn't want her to lock them out. Waferr glared at him and then handed them over. She followed WPC Smythe out of the house and Knowles locked up before handing the keys to Smythe for safekeeping. They walked over to the car park and Knowles made sure Waferr was secure in the back of the police car before he left them. He walked back over the road and into Goat Parva's shop.

As the bell sounded Brenda Jargoy came out from the back of the shop – she had been crying.

"Can I help you? Oh it's you, Inspector – more nicotine patches for you?"

"Where's Tom, Brenda – and don't say you don't know?"

"He's not around – he's gone out in his van."

"Did he go out this morning, Brenda?"

"Tom is always in and out, Inspector, he's not your regular 9 to 5 man."

"So he was out early this morning was he?"

"I was asleep."

"Not you as well! Why do the people of Goat Parva cause me problems even when they're asleep? Have you seen him this morning, Brenda?"

"Not to speak to. I did hear him going out around 7:30 – he left in the van and that's what woke me up. He's not been back since then."

"What has upset you, Brenda?"

"The time of life I suppose. I get very weepy these days."

"It's not connected with your visit to Langstroth Hall earlier this morning then? Did you find Lord Avon was indisposed?"

Brenda Jargoy looked wounded – the truth hurt.

"Are you spying on me – that's police harassment isn't it?"

"I was simply observing the goings on in the village as part of our investigation into the three murders that have happened here recently."

"I didn't see you – where were you?"

"I was hiding in plain sight." He gripped his stomach. "Hard to believe I know – anyway, I have to go and visit Barry Janus in the hospital – he was attacked this morning by person or persons unknown at this point in time."

"And you suspect Tom of doing this wicked crime – do you think he's the murderer?"

Knowles didn't tell Brenda Jargoy that Barry Janus was still alive and nor did he say that he didn't think Tom Jargoy was a suspect in the murders.

"Tom, your husband, is a person of interest – be sure to mention this to him when he next pops into your life. He can come to the station if he wants or we can come back here again to interview him."

"I will tell him – he's not a murderer."

"Thank you – oh there's one final thing I wanted to ask – do you have any Rohypnol in the house?"

"What? No we don't have any of that in the medicine cabinet."

"That's what I thought – it was just something Carly Waferr mentioned earlier. Not to worry. Cheerio."

"Carly Waferr – why would she have mentioned Rohypnol in connection with us?"

Knowles didn't hear the question as he was on his way out of the shop – he had certainly mentioned a few interesting subjects to Brenda Jargoy, which would make the next conversation between the Jargoys a very spicy and tempestuous one. He hoped so anyway as he needed people to start telling him what they actually knew about events in Goat Parva.

Chapter 8

Saturday, afternoon

At the hospital Barry Janus had just awoken from his unconscious state. He looked around him and then winced at the pain from his wound, which had been cleaned and dressed. He saw the nurse and also two people who looked vaguely familiar. They were the police who'd tried to keep him at home, but he'd evaded them even if it was just for five minutes.

"Welcome back, Barry – how are you feeling?"

"What's your name, I can't remember – it's not Knowles is it?"

"It's not Knowles – he will be along soon he assures me – my name is Barnes. You escaped and then got knocked on the head didn't you? Who was it, who did it, Barry?"

"You're going to have to believe me when I tell you that I don't know who it was. I was in the woods and someone thumped me from the side and I fell down. All I could see was part of the church and I crawled and stumbled towards it but I fell over the stile and must have passed out again."

"Do you know who found you?"

"Not a clue – who was it?"

"It was Reverend Strong, we believe, that was what the dispatcher was told, but the Reverend's now disappeared."

"I can't help you, officer, I can't help you."

"Where were you going, Barry, with your bag of toiletries and spare clothes?"

"I was going to find a boat to head to Leicester and then catch a bus up to Lancashire where my sister lives in a place called Billinge – it's near Wigan."

"Find a boat, Barry? You mean borrow one? Never to return it."

"Yes, I do mean that – just a rowing boat, mind, nothing major."

"Why were you running away and who from?"

"I was running away because I didn't want to be murdered – I am not sure who the murderer is, but they've killed the other three people in my group and they've had a go at me now, so they're bound to try again."

"You weren't attacked by the murderer, Barry; the murderer would have killed you and taken your possessions so that we wouldn't have found them."

"Well that's reassuring – I am a victim of a general mugging without purpose rather than being targeted by a serial killer – I feel deflated now."

"Has anyone threatened you recently, Barry?"

"Well plenty of people; if you carry a tripod with you for photographic purposes and you live in Goat Parva then everyone assumes you're a stalker – so the list would include Lord Avon, Carly Waferr, Rev Strong, Lady Avon, and Brenda Jargoy."

"That's most of Goat Parva, Barry, why are you so unpopular?"

"It's a gift I have I suppose – I notice things and am always hanging around the woods observing them going about their business as it were."

"Whose business have you observed recently?"

"That'd be Carly Waferr meeting Tom Jargoy in those woods a few days ago – she swore that she'd get even with me and, wait a moment, Tom Jargoy also threatened me a few days ago – he'd probably be the last one actually."

"Tom Jargoy? Why did he do that?"

"Because I know where his wife goes for her pleasures and I know that Tom Jargoy and Carly Waferr are regularly in each other's arms."

"Why would he choose to threaten you now, Barry, those affairs have been going on for years."

"They have, but I think Clem Shapiro's murder upset the equilibrium of the village somewhat and everyone felt threatened. In Goat Parva, everyone is up to something that's not on the level and yet everything still appeared to be normal – once Shapiro was killed people started asking questions about who was where and with whom and the mood changed a little bit." The mention of murder had brought Barry's headache back and he winced in pain. To increase the pressure on Janus, Knowles chose this moment to enter the room.

Barnes nodded to Knowles and continued, "That's a good observation, Barry – what people thought was normal behaviour has been shown to be anything but and everyone has become ill-at-ease with what they're doing and what other people have been doing."

At this point Barry Janus suddenly felt very tired and he pressed the button to attract the attention of the nurse. She came into the room and suggested that they should continue their questioning the following day as he needed rest.

As Knowles and Barnes left the hospital a thought suddenly struck Barnes.

"Just before you came in, sir, Barry listed out all the people who had threatened him recently and very interesting it was too. He said that Brenda Jargoy, Lady Avon, and, get this, Reverend Strong had threatened him."

"Why would our esteemed vicar threaten anyone? What was he up to? The two women I can understand, but not him. What I really don't understand is this – why would Rev Strong report Barry to the ambulance people and then disappear?"

"My guess would be that Rev Strong didn't phone the dispatcher, but someone else did, perhaps after a fit of guilt?"

"A fit of guilt – doesn't sound like anyone I am familiar with around here."

"Those phone calls are recorded so perhaps we could listen in and see who it was that phoned."

"That's a great idea, Barnesy, especially as we know that the name Reverend Strong was mentioned by the person phoning up. You might need a warrant, so obtain one now and then head over to the dispatch centre."

"You said just now that you could understand why Lady Avon and Brenda Jargoy would threaten Barry Janus – could you tell me why?"

"Yes, Brenda Jargoy is seeing Lord Avon and has been

for years – in fact Wendy Jargoy might well be his daughter, in which case Poppy Avon and Wendy are half-sisters. So if Barry is snooping around Langstroth Hall he's bound to have seen Brenda going about her business and perhaps she thought he would tell her husband, but I think he already knows, but perhaps she thought she would threaten Barry as everyone else in the village has. Lady Avon has seen all the stalkers around the Baker-Clements' place. She knows what Barry is like, and therefore feels, quite rightly in my humble opinion, that Barry is not a suitable role model for her son, Claude. On the other hand, Barry could be laying it on with a trowel and exaggerating to make himself appear more important than he actually is."

"I'll go and get that warrant," said Barnes his head spinning with the complicated affairs in Goat Parva.

"Good idea, Barnesy."

Barnes headed over to the police station and Knowles then took a call from WPC Smythe as he sat in his car.

"Hello – so the test has been done…I thought coffee was a diuretic…she's full of it…so it's negative for rohypnol, but there's some other strange substances which require further analysis and a blood test…OK may as well appear to be thorough I suppose. If she wants a lawyer she can have one…by all means – how about conspiracy to commit murder that will do for a start, perverting the course of justice, for dessert and perhaps something meatier for the main course such as attempted murder. Thank you."

As Knowles rang off the green handset indicator on his phone appeared again and he swiped his finger across the screen – he didn't particularly like unknown calls.

"Hello is that Inspector Knowles, can I speak to him please?" said a rather posh voice that sounded slightly inebriated.

"You're speaking to him."

"Oh, Inspector, how different you sound on the phone than in real life, it's Antonia Avon, Inspector, and I have some information for you. Now you remember that I said I saw someone but I didn't remember who, well I do remember now. I am still unsure of the name however I do know that they are a friend of Wendy Jargoy, that bat-faced girl who lives at the shop."

"How do you know she's a friend of Wendy Jargoy's – you must have seen them together at some point?"

"Yes, I saw them at the odd animal shelter in Madeley Waterless, not together but they both worked there I know."

"And you are sure you don't know the name?"

"It might have been Tamsin or Jasmine or something similar."

"I think the choice is Yasmin or Andrea, if memory serves me right."

"Then it will be Yasmin that I saw."

"And could you point her out at an identity parade, if that became necessary?"

"I suppose I could, as long as it was early in the morning. I am more of a morning person."

Knowles smiled to himself and wondered when she started to drink in the morning.

"It would be at a time to suit you of course, Lady Avon. But we will cross that wagon I mean bridge when we have to do so."

"Thank you, Inspector Knowles I appreciate your accommodation of my request."

"Thank you, Lady Avon, for the call. Goodbye for now."

Well, well, what was Yasmin doing on that night, experiencing being a stalker for one night or something more sinister such as checking the lie of the land for the future? thought Knowles as he headed home to see how Gemma the cat had been in his absence. *Gemma's probably sitting on the kitchen counter admiring the birds through the window.*

============

At the same time as Knowles was heading home, Tom Jargoy had returned to his home to be met by a tearful Brenda.

"What have you been doing today, Tom, the police have been around here twice looking for you in connection with an attack on Barry Janus and also accusing you of using

Rohypnol on Carly Waferr. Why would they think you'd do either of those things? Where have you been?"

"I went for a walk in the woods this morning, if you must know, and I did see Carly coming from Hen's Wood but I have no idea what Rohypnol is – does it help with joint pain or something like that?"

"It's a sedative similar to a sleeping pill that's used on date rapes a lot according to the newspapers."

"And when was I supposed to have administered this sedative to Carly? When I was walking behind her at a distance of 50 yards?"

"The police want to see you about raping her I presume or having sex without her consent."

"I was nowhere near her – as for the other thing you said, I take it someone has attacked Barry Janus? Is he dead?"

"I think he might be, although the inspector didn't say categorically. Did you have anything to do with it, Tom Jargoy?"

"I had nothing to do with it, but I am not too distraught about the attack – he's had it coming to him for years with his stalking ways; I wonder if it's the same murderer as the other three people? Does this make it four murders?"

"If he's dead then yes it does – so have you killed the others too?"

"I haven't killed anyone, you've forgotten that we were together when Pig Boy got killed and the police believe, so I understand, that the same person killed all the murder victims."

"Perhaps I was your alibi for that murder and your Carly accomplice did it and you committed the others?"

"Carly is not my accomplice for anything – she hasn't got it in her to harm anyone; she says a prayer before cutting the mushrooms out of the ground in the woods, how sensitive is that?"

"How do you know that, Tom Jargoy; you've been in those woods with her I presume?"

"I heard that is what she did – actually I heard that from Barry Janus, so I suppose he does have his uses."

"What reporting on people's mushroom cutting

techniques? Why would you be gossiping about such trivial things?"

"I can't tell people what they should talk to me about – he just came out with it one day, didn't he? I can't wear a placard with all the subjects I don't want people to talk to me about written on it."

"You're just trivialising things now like you always do; if you don't contact the police then I will do so on your behalf – you have some explaining to do, Tom Jargoy."

With that Brenda Jargoy flounced out of the room, grabbed her coat, and left her house. She needed to get some fresh air down by the river. Tom Jargoy frowned – he was in a tight spot.

============

Knowles had found Gemma sitting on the kitchen window sill facing inwards and looking upset. There had not been enough food in her bowl and she was angry with her staff member for starving her – at least that was Knowles' interpretation of her behaviour. He was just cleaning out her litter tray when his phone rang – it was Sergeant Barnes.

"What are you up to, sir?"

"Well, Barnesy, I suppose you could say I am doing the same as I do at work except that this is more literally correct, though perhaps more satisfying because I am actually achieving something and I am benefiting another living creature and perhaps my neighbours too as their gardens are safe from being dug up by my cat looking for somewhere to crap in private. I bet you're glad you asked now."

"I am always glad that I asked you a question, sir, because you always give such captivating answers."

"You will go far, Sergeant, perhaps even to the Orion Nebula."

"Interstellar travel is not on my agenda just yet, but back to more earthly matters – the voice on the message to the dispatcher is not Reverend Strong, but it does seem rather familiar and I can't quite place the accent."

"OK, when I have stopped sifting cat litter I will come

over to the station – do they have a number of the phone that was used?"

"It's the public phone box outside St Timothy's church."

"Who would have been in the churchyard and wanted to cover their tracks by using a public phone?"

"Could it have been the attacker?"

"In this fit of guilt you believe criminals have?"

"Well it is possible – could the attacker have hit Barry too hard and felt sorry for him?"

"I really don't think so, the attack took place in Hen's Wood and the attacker left Barry's bag in a tree stump – what you're suggesting is that the attacker hit Barry in the woods, followed him to the church, and then felt sorry and phoned the emergency services. Why would they wait to feel sorry? The person who phoned 999 must have known that Barry was in the churchyard mustn't they? They must have found him there rather than followed him there. The attacker didn't know Barry would crawl anywhere let alone St Timothy's church."

"I see your point, sir."

"Good – and I will be with you in a few minutes."

===========

Knowles found Barnes hunched over a recording device at his desk.

"Do you have a better idea of who phoned the emergency services?"

"Let's listen to it on the loudspeakers, shall we?"

Barnes pressed the button and the message was played. "Hello, emergency services, please send an ambulance to the back of St Timothy's church – the graveyard, where I have just seen a body… no one that's not meant to be there, the man is still alive and above ground… my name… I am the Reverend Strong and I should go and minister to his needs. Bye."

"Any ideas, sir?"

"Well it's not Tom Jargoy, Lord Avon, Claude Avon, Mr Greggs or Kev at the pub – it's not Barry and it's not either you or me. It's not Reverend Strong as I am sure he would have said 'tend to his needs' rather than 'minister to his needs' given that he's a Reverend and not a Minister. So... it's either a complete stranger that knows Reverend Strong..."

"...His name is on the church sign, sir, near the phone box..."

"...Or it's that idiot postman Tim Armstrong on his morning round."

"Why would he be delivering in the churchyard?"

"I think the church has a postbox on that side of the church, so he might have good reason to be there now I come to think of it."

"We should check with the reverend to see whether he received any post today."

"If we can find him – and we should because we need to know why he threatened Barry J."

"I can't think what Barry would have seen him doing..."

"...Or who with for that matter unless it was Carol Herald."

"He did say she was a good friend to the church, which could be a euphemism of course. It could also just be the truth, which is something we have to remember."

"Yes, he could have been telling the truth, which would make him quite unique around here. Anyway, Barnesy, we should take a trip over to the animal sanctuary at Madeley and see the wonderful Yasmin, who was identified by Lady Avon earlier today as the person she saw through a telescope at the stalking session a couple of weeks ago. This will be the last action of the day."

"Speak for yourself, sir."

"I was doing, Sergeant."

As they drove over to Madeley Waterless the two officers discussed how best to apprehend Tim Armstrong and agreed to wait until the end of his round on Monday.

Knowles parked his vehicle in the shelter's yard and they headed to the reception. Wendy Jargoy was sweeping up some manure and the officers said hello.

"Are you here to see Andrea?" asked Wendy.

"No, Yasmin, is she around?" asked Knowles.

"She's over by the stables I think."

"How come you're sweeping up wearing just one glove?"

"We lost the other one a few days ago; it disappeared overnight."

"I am the same with socks," smiled Knowles, "they just disappear in the drawer somehow."

Knowles and Barnes headed to the stables and saw a rather lovely ginger-haired girl brushing a horse with great gusto. This must be Yasmin though she didn't fit Lady Avon's description too well. What she did fit, exactly, was the image that Knowles and Barnes had found at PC Davis' house – the hair was longer and the clothes were shabbier, but the face was a match.

"Yasmin? My name is Inspector Colin Knowles and this is Sergeant Barnes, we'd like to ask you a few questions."

"I've been expecting you, officers – Andrea said you'd be over today to ask me some questions and you've just about made it in time."

"What's the name of the horse?" asked Barnes.

"You didn't come all this way to ask me that did you, Sergeant? His name's Edgar, you can ask me another question if they're all that easy."

Barnes blushed slightly – Yasmin had a very engaging personality he found.

"My question doesn't relate to the horsey," said Knowles, "I'd like to know where you were the night Clem Shapiro was murdered over in Goat Parva."

"I am pretty sure I was at the Red Lion in Flixton with my boyfriend, Toby, Toby Philpott, for most of the evening and then home to bed."

"And Toby, Toby Philpott can verify this of course?"

"I am sure he can do that for you, Inspector; he works at the charity shop in Flixton."

"He does, doesn't he. I have met him before a few years ago – possession of a narcotic I seem to remember."

"That's good then that you've met – I won't have to introduce you two."

"What about Thursday morning and Friday morning – do

you have an alibi for those days round about 7am?"

"Friday mornings I go running so that's where I'd be somewhere along the river perhaps at that time; Thursday I'd be asleep I would think."

"Anyone else around at the time?"

"Friday morning – I thought I saw Barry Janus in the woods at one point, but I could never be sure if it was him or Claude Avon as they were always carrying around a similar looking tripod."

"You saw the tripod but not the man?"

"I did I suppose – I just didn't want to be photographed by them; they are both creepy people."

"There's a word for that isn't there – when you use part of something to describe the whole – such as describing 50 ships as '50 sail'?"

"I am sure there is, Inspector."

"Isn't the word 'unobservant'?" smiled Barnes.

"It's something like sin-ek-ter-gee, but written synecdoche I think," scowled Knowles, trying to remember the crossword from last Sunday's newspaper.

"Is it treatable?" wondered Yasmin.

"If poetry is treatable then yes it is," grinned Knowles, "it's used often in poetry to aid description."

"I don't read poetry," said Yasmin, "I don't really have the time."

"Not even when you went stalking with Carol Herald a couple of weeks ago?"

"What were we stalking and when?" asked Yasmin.

"You were seen outside the home of Lord and Lady Avon two Tuesdays ago late at night in the company of Carol Herald and I believe you were going to watch Danica Baker-Clements."

"That tart! Why would I do that? Was she having sex with someone – actually she's almost always having sex from what I was told – no I was not there."

Yasmin stopped brushing Edgar and stared at Inspector Knowles daring him to break eye contact. Barnes happened to know that the Inspector practiced this technique with his cat Gemma who never blinked, so he was rather good at it.

"Yasmin, do you remember PC Roger Davis – did he bring his dog here with him?" asked Barnes.

"Yes, he did – it wasn't a police dog – it was his dog and he mistreated it terribly; Carol used to shout at him."

"I find that really odd, because they went stalking together quite often."

"I couldn't comment on that – Carol had these Jekyll and Hyde relationships with men, such as the Pig Man Shapiro, and with Reverend Strong, and yet she hated butchers and religion – well she said she did, actions speak louder than words I suppose."

"Indeed they do, Yasmin," said Knowles. "If Carol's relationships were indeed Jekyll and Hyde then could she have killed Shapiro do you think? And PC Davis?"

"She did become very angry with people on occasions when she thought they were deliberately mistreating their pets."

"Getting very angry is not that far from murdering someone would you say?"

"Combining the anger with opportunity might be enough I suppose," said Yasmin thoughtfully.

"Do you ever get really angry, Yasmin?"

"I tend not to because I always feel there's something I can do instead of getting angry – again actions are the best option to alleviate your anger; anger is borne out of frustration that you can't do anything to help."

"Do you act in anger though, Yasmin?"

"I act because I want to avoid being angry – I act to make things better."

"I see – well that's revealing, thank you. Is Andrea around today?"

"She's not around today – it's her day off; just the two of us today."

"She wasn't here this morning then?"

"No – off for the whole day."

"Right, by the way – when you said that Carol Herald had a Jekyll and Hyde relationship with Reverend Strong what did you mean?"

"Carol despised religion, organised religion, and yet she

grew vegetables for the church's events – Rev Strong was always very grateful of course, but I was always surprised Carol provided excess food to the church rather than to the food bank for example."

"Was there an element of coercion do you think?"

"Coercion is a little strong – my guess would be he knew something about her that she didn't want to be revealed."

"Any ideas as to what that would be?" enquired Barnes.

"Perhaps relating to her stalking activities; he might have realised she was one of the stalkers a long time ago."

"I didn't think the stalkers had been going that long – only about three months."

"I wouldn't know – I really wouldn't know."

"Did you ever notice a change in her general demeanour in the past few months?"

"Well now you come to mention it, she did seem rather introverted for a few days about three months ago and did get really upset with people for no apparent reason."

"I see – well we shall have to speak to Reverend Strong about this and see what he says. Thank you for the information you have provided, Yasmin; we should be on our way." Knowles wanted to leave the animal shelter straightaway and swiftly brought the conversation to an end.

"That was very interesting," said Knowles, as he kangaroo-hopped his vehicle through the entrance gate. "Oopps, grit in the petrol again, so, firstly the stalker in the woods this morning must have been Andrea as she isn't in work today and they wouldn't leave just one person on duty here. Secondly, why is Yasmin trying to make Carol Herald out to be an ogre and trying to make us think that Carol was the murderer? Of the first two victims of course; she hasn't said it in so many words, but she's trying to pin the blame on Carol."

"While at the same time trying to give us the impression there's a wide range of people who would like to have got rid of Carol."

"What do you reckon, Barnesy, Carol killed Pig Boy and PC Davis and then gets a smack on the head herself?"

"No, the MO was the same in all three cases and there's not a chance that a different murderer could have known how the first two people were killed, as we didn't tell anyone how they died; a smack on the head is as much as we have said to anyone."

"Yes, there's a number of different ways of doing it of course."

"The third thing we have learned is that only Yasmin and Wendy were here today, so when the Waferr woman was heading here she must have wanted to see one or the other of those two," mused Barnes.

"So why would Carly Waferr have to let one of them, or both of course, know that Adelaide Hills' phone had been lost?"

"My guess is both as it relates to some animal rights protest rather than one individual who is the murderer."

"Tell you what let's see if a night in the cells helps Waferr remember more clearly what happened this morning. Let's see her tomorrow morning at 9am and then head over to Goat Parva and intercept Tim Armstrong on his round and ask him about his impression of a man of the cloth."

"Sounds like a plan, sir."

"Yes, I think we are getting closer to finding out who murdered those three people."

Chapter 9

Sunday, 8:50am

Barnes walked into the office and saw that Knowles was eating an apple at his desk.

"No full English breakfast for you today, sir?"

"No, absolutely not, just fruit and a cup of Earl Grey tea sweetened with honey; I think this diet is working – I have lost a pound since the start of it and I just have to keep going."

"Have you started to exercise too, because that will really help to burn off the calories? There's a gym down the street and we get special rates there, you should attack the weight from both sides as it were."

"Right, well I will have to think about that, of course, as exercise is anathema to me and has been for most of my life. Well, not most, all really, but it's time to change I think, even walking up the stairs will help rather than taking the lift won't it?"

"Every little helps, sir, and it is better to start off slowly and increase the intensity."

"Right, well that's also true of interrogations, so let's go and see that Waferr woman and find out what she says for herself."

The cells were two floors down and Knowles instinctively pressed the down arrow on the lift; Barnes indicated the stairs and Knowles smiled to himself; this was going to take time.

Barnes arrived at Room 3 and looked through the toughened glass – Waferr was in there already with her lawyer. He opened the door and left it for Knowles. He switched on the recording device and read out the time, date, and those present which now included a slightly wheezing Knowles.

"Are you alright, Inspector Knowles?" asked Carly Waferr.

Knowles nodded and indicated that Barnes should start the interview.

"Carly Waferr – yesterday morning you tried to find a phone in Culpepper's Woods and when you were unable to find it, you headed in the direction of Madeley Waterless. You claimed yesterday that you were sleepwalking and didn't know where you were heading; is this still your story or have you had a chance to revise this story and, if so, what would you like to tell us?"

Carly Waferr looked at her lawyer who nodded.

"Sergeant Barnes – I have had a good night's sleep and I seem to have found some clarifications regarding my story; I was asked by someone at the animal shelter in Madeley Waterless to help them in a small matter namely to steal the mobile phone of Adelaide Hills so that she couldn't use it to report a crime that she might come across during her morning walks. The idea was I believe, that she would have to go home and phone the police from there thus giving the perpetrators of the crime enough time to make their escape from the scene."

"What was the scene of the crime going to be?"

"That was not shared with me; you have to believe me there."

"Somewhere where Adelaide Hills and her dog were going to discover the criminals at work; but at work doing what – those two don't walk that far really and why the emphasis on not being apprehended rather than not being identified?"

"They'd be wearing balaclavas I suppose and overalls."

"Where though – if Adelaide Hills would see them then surely someone else would see them too; where would Adelaide Hills go that no one else goes to?"

"Something on the river, what about something on the river, the animal research farm is by the river, and if they were planning on getting into the research farm then the river is the best way."

Knowles cleared his throat slightly.

"If the element of time is so important then it would be best served by them getting away from the farm downstream;

126

Adelaide Hills wouldn't know where they'd landed if they were getting away as she would have gone home to use her phone – with her mobile phone she could just watch them and tell the police the landing place. The thieves were getting away with animals in a form of rescue."

"Did you actually get to the animal shelter, Carly?"

"No, Andrea stopped me; told me to go back home through the woods."

"Did you tell her about the phone?"

"I didn't, Inspector, I was specifically told not to tell Andrea about the phone."

"Who by?"

"Carol, Carol Herald, she asked me to steal the phone and not to tell Andrea."

"So why were you heading to the shelter if you knew Carol was dead?"

Carly Waferr looked at her lawyer.

"Because, I assumed, I assumed, that the other two, Yasmin and Wendy, were in the know – Carol didn't say that I shouldn't tell them like she specifically did with Andrea. I didn't know Andrea was in the woods that morning."

"This just gets worse; Carol, Wendy, and Yasmin were planning to break in to the animal research farm, steal animals, float downstream, release the animals or look after them at least, and yet Andrea wasn't to know presumably because she would disapprove of their scheme. You've also confirmed that the thread we found in the woods that morning was from some tracksuit bottoms worn by Andrea. Thank you for that."

"That's good, Barnesy, but the problem is that Andrea would see the extra animals at the shelter, so I doubt they would look after the animals themselves; they'd pass them on to someone else for safekeeping or for publicity purposes."

"When did Carol ask you to steal the phone, Carly?"

"The day before Clem Shapiro was killed – I stole the phone the morning that Clem's body was found; it was recharging in her lounge and I took the whole lot and continued my walk past the church and into Hen's Wood that way. You can imagine my surprise when I saw her on the

127

walk and I had her phone under the mushrooms in my basket. I almost fainted."

"Why did you have to steal the phone?"

"Because I don't agree with the experiments at the farm and I wanted to help in my own way, and I am a neighbour of Adelaide's and I am always around leaving her mushrooms and other gifts. She doesn't lock her lounge door when she goes out with Bingo the dog."

"Why did you take it with you into the woods yesterday morning?"

"It was in the jacket I was wearing – I hid it there after Clem's body was found; I put the other wires and things into a bag because Carol said I should return everything once she'd let me know the coast was clear – of course she never did. I was going to place everything in Bingo's kennel."

"You were going to frame the dog? Implicate the retriever in the crime? Planting evidence!" Knowles laughed out loud.

"I wonder when the crime was going to take place – when were they planning to raid the farm? They took a risk though, because Mrs Hills could have easily replaced her mobile phone," said Barnes.

"No chance of that happening, Sergeant, Adelaide is a little tight with money, shall we say, and would hunt high and low for the phone for weeks rather than buy another one."

"Really? You know her well then."

"I think so – she would blame Bingo for the missing phone and would be convinced that he'd buried it somewhere." Carly Waferr smiled.

"I am sure that's the case – Mrs Hills told us that Bingo had buried the phone in the garden somewhere and she would find it eventually," said Barnes.

"And of course she would have," smirked Knowles, "in his kennel."

Carly Waferr reddened slightly and her lawyer asked whether the interview was now at an end. Knowles nodded and Barnes switched off the recording device. Carly Waferr would be allowed to go home as long as she didn't try to leave the village of Goat Parva.

Barnes took the stairs two at a time, whereas Knowles plodded up more slowly but at least he didn't use the lift. They both wrote down their findings from the interview and then headed to the car park.

As they headed to Goat Parva in Knowles' Land Rover they discussed what they had just heard. Knowles began.

"Do you believe what Carly Waferr said about Carol Herald organising something criminal – it needn't be related to the research farm, it's just that was all I could think of?"

"Could it be related to what actually happened – the murder I mean; if Carol was planning on killing Clem then everything worked out really well because she wasn't found at the crime scene?"

"You mean she was being ultra-cautious by having Carly steal the phone?"

"The only problem then is that Clem was killed around 11pm, approximately 8 hours before Mrs Hills goes for a walk with Bingo."

"It must have been something that Carol was planning on doing in the early morning when she knew Adelaide was going to be around therefore it must be something to do with the research farm by the river."

"Do you think Reverend Strong could have found out about this plan somehow and Carol tried to buy him off with food parcels?"

"How would the vicar have found out about a plan to rescue animals from a research farm? He wouldn't move in the same circles would he?"

As they went round a bend they passed a cyclist – it was Tim Armstrong heading towards Goat Parva.

"That was Tim Armstrong, I should accelerate and get to Goat Parva ahead of him and hide this jalopy; we can question him now, not tomorrow."

"Where's he delivering today?" wondered Barnes.

"Danica's – anyway you were going to say?"

"Well, Carol and the Reverend did know each other and he did act on her behalf when I went around to her house and she arrived and he warned her off, so he has a history of helping and protecting her."

"True enough – perhaps he expressed a view that indicated he was against animal cruelty, Carol told him she was planning a raid and then he said he couldn't approve of anyone breaking the law. Perhaps that's how it went and she felt guilty about burdening him with the information and in order to assuage her conscience she offered him food for his flock."

"That's a distinct possibility, sir – but doesn't that show Carol couldn't be our murderer? If she was of that inclination, wouldn't she have knocked the Reverend on the head and then her little secret would have been buried with him?"

"You could well be right there, Sergeant; I wonder where the Reverend has gone; perhaps we should visit him in his church? Talking of which, there it is in the distance. Let's get this thing hidden, so Tim doesn't see it."

"When we question him – do you think he will admit it?"

"Is it a criminal offence?"

"Impersonating a vicar? Well I think it can be under certain circumstances, but I am not sure this is one of those occasions."

"Giving false information when ringing the emergency services; isn't that illegal?"

"It sounds good to me – let's see what Tim believes."

They parked in the car park of the Badger & Ferret and waited. Knowles parked his vehicle in such a way that people coming along Leicester Road from the south wouldn't see him until they were almost on top of him. The plan was to follow Armstrong and apprehend him at the top of the Baker-Clements' drive. After 5 minutes the smiling visage of Tim Armstrong came pedalling along, but then he turned into Sharrock Lane and parked his bike at Number 3 the home of Mr Greggs. He went through the gate and down the path to the door.

When he returned he found two people closely inspecting his bike.

"Why are you delivering on a Sunday, Tim – don't you get a day off?"asked Barnes.

"It was a special delivery for Mr Greggs. He wasn't in

yesterday when I called, and won't be tomorrow either, so I thought I would deliver it today just as a favour. Anyway, what are you doing with my bike; that is the property of the Royal Mail."

"Is that right – so it doesn't belong to Reverend Strong then?"

"Has he reported his bike missing?"

"He hasn't reported his bike missing; however he has requested an ambulance be sent to St Timothy's church because he had found a body in the churchyard. However, there was something odd about this – any ideas what that might be Tim?"

"A body in the churchyard – that's a joke I suppose?"

"No, Tim, the odd thing was that Reverend Strong didn't make that call – I am wondering whether you can help us find out who did make that call."

"How could I help? You're the police you find out – I don't expect you to deliver my mail for me."

"I think Tim is getting stroppy, Sergeant, what do you think?" interjected Knowles.

"I think Tim doesn't know that all emergency services phone calls are recorded. And that we can listen to those calls. And that we can identify who made those calls from the voices. And we know it was you, Tim, who made that call, so why not just admit it?"

"Oh that call, yes I remember that now."

"…Do you know it's illegal to give false information in calls to the emergency services?"

"I didn't know that, no, I thought it was more important to order the ambulance for the man who was injured than give my name – I still had my round to finish and couldn't be delayed."

"And you gave Reverend Strong's name for what reason exactly, Tim?"

"I was outside the church and assumed he would be round when the ambulance arrived – I wouldn't have been around would I?"

"Did you recognise the man who was injured?"

"I did recognise him – he was the man from next to the

church called Barry Janus – he'd been hit on the head and had bled a lot, but he was still conscious."

"Did you see anyone else around the churchyard, Tim, was there anybody lurking in the woods that you saw?"

"I didn't see anyone in the woods at all nor in the churchyard; there was nobody around."

"Did he say anything to you when you found him?"

"I thought he mumbled something like 'why did she do this' but I couldn't be sure."

" 'Why did she do this' – what on earth does that mean?"

"Are you sure he said 'she', Tim?"

"It wasn't 'he' – it was 'she'"

"Thank you, Tim," said Knowles, "please consider yourself cautioned however regarding impersonation of a vicar of the church – if you ever discover another body around here tell the dispatch people it's you that's reporting the problem."

Tim Armstrong nodded, sprang onto his bike, and cycled off towards the church.

Knowles looked at Barnes and shook his head.

"Just when you think this case is close to being solved, something comes along that shows you don't know what's going on at all. What on earth would Barry Janus mean by 'why did she do this'?"

"Well, we only have Tim's word for this phrase being used; he may have misheard Barry – and even if he's heard correctly does the 'do' necessarily refer to hitting Barry on the head?"

"We have to go and visit our Barry again and ask him what he meant by this. I think he's referring to Carol Herald starting this stalking group a few months ago; he's regretting being part of it and is blaming her for his own weakness. At least that's what I guess and I hope otherwise it would mean that Barry thought he'd been attacked by a woman."

"He might have been, sir, but you don't believe that."

"This is an opportunist crime and not one committed by the murderer; someone must have seen our Barry stealing out of his house and followed him or saw him down by the river and thought this was a good time for revenge."

"What about Reverend Strong? Where is he now?"

"Let's go and have a look in the church, Sergeant; perhaps he's gone for a visit to his superiors to confess something to them."

"I wasn't aware that his sort confessed."

"Anglicans don't no, but perhaps he will deal in hypothetical situations and seek guidance regarding what should be done if someone were to tell him something that suggested the law was going to be broken, for example."

"Isn't that a personal matter rather than a religious opinion?"

"Depends on your faith, Sergeant – personal feelings become subservient to the religion at some point."

"Right…oh who's this?"

A brown van pulled up beside them and Tom Jargoy hit his head on the window before rolling it down completely.

"Inspector, Brenda didn't come home last night, she went out for a walk to the river late in the afternoon and that was the last I saw of her. I have been down there this morning and walked both ways and I have not seen any trace of her."

"Not another one – did she have any reason not to come back; did you two argue?" asked Knowles.

"We had words, yes."

"What words exactly were used? Assault, sex, mysterious goings on in the woods, rohypnol?"

"Quite a few more than that actually; she told me you'd been looking for me and that I was a suspect in the death of Barry Janus. She told me to contact you, which is what I am doing indirectly."

"I think Brenda has forced your hand Tom and your demeanour does rather show that you still care for her."

"Of course I do."

"You can't mean that – you were shagging Carly Waferr in the woods yesterday morning," said Barnes. "Anyway, I suppose I should report your dearly beloved as missing – what was she wearing?"

Tom Jargoy gave a sketchy description to Barnes, while Knowles phoned the hospital to see if Barry Janus was awake, which he was and so could see them to answer further questions.

"Right," said Barnes, "two constables are going to search the riverbank and Hen's Wood, the very same area as was searched yesterday. However, they will be looking for a different person today." He shook his head in bewilderment.

Knowles smiled. "Tom, park your vehicle and come with me and the sergeant to Scoresby station, as we need to find out some details of your activities yesterday."

"What activities?"

"All of them, Tom – every single one, you were a busy boy, weren't you?"

"I don't know what you mean."

As Jargoy drove to his house and parked, Knowles told Barnes to interrogate Jargoy along with WPC Smythe and see what he knew about the attack on Barry Janus. Tom Jargoy must not be told about Janus still being alive. Knowles would go and visit Barry Janus and ask him what he had meant by the phrase that was heard by Tim Armstrong. If Jargoy asked, Knowles was 'filing a report'."

Knowles drove back to Scoresby with Barnes and Jargoy in the back. Not many words passed between them until they saw Carly Waferr's brown van chugging towards them.

"Where's she been?" said Jargoy.

"She's been in the cells overnight, Tom, for questioning and for tests to establish whether she was given Rohypnol yesterday morning, while she was sleep walking around Goat Parva."

"Sleep walking – when was she doing that?"

"All morning, well at least in the early morning when she was in the woods and lost the phone she was keeping for the girls at the animal shelter."

"Which girls at the shelter, which ones – do you mean Wendy?"

"Yes, definitely – Wendy and her friends were planning a raid we think on the research farm in the early morning in the near future. Do you know anything, Tom?"

"What would I know?" asked Tom.

"You might have noticed some strange behaviour from

Wendy, staying out late, getting up early, wearing overalls, getting her hair cut shorter than normal."

"She did all those things as a matter of course."

"Did she ever mention any other animal shelters in the area that she had visited or people she'd met?"

"She mentioned a few at times: Norwich, Northampton, Nottingham…"

"…Any that didn't begin with the letter 'N'?"

"Not that I can remember, no."

"Well if you can think of any do let the sergeant here know."

"I will, Inspector, don't worry."

"Right, I won't then, here we are, gentlemen. Sergeant please escort Mr Jargoy to an interview room. I have some tedious paperwork to do and I will see you later."

Knowles watched Barnes and Jargoy disappear into the police station. He almost switched on the ignition again, but decided to walk over to the hospital; he might lose a few more calories that way.

At reception the admin assistant checked with Janus' nurse that he was awake and able to see the police. Knowles was given the go ahead and shown to an open ward where Janus had been moved that morning. Knowles closed the curtains around Janus and sat quite close to him; he didn't want to shout at Barry, not just yet anyway.

"Barry – I have been speaking to your knight in shining armour, the good Samaritan who rescued you from your predicament."

"Who was it – Reverend Strong?"

"Why do you say that?"

"I was in the churchyard and that's where you normally find vicars more than any other profession."

"Really – I didn't know that - well that's not the case this time, you were found by the postman, Tim Armstrong."

"What was he doing there; he's normally at Danica Baker-Clements' house?"

"Well not this time, this time he was helping you, Barry, and he said that when he first found you, you said this phrase 'why did she do this'? Can you shed any light on what you

135

meant when you said 'why did she do this'? Who were you referring to? Who is the 'she' Barry?"

"Is he sure I said that?"

Knowles nodded.

"Well, I don't know who hit me, so I can't have been referring to that person. My guess would be that I was referring to the stalking group and that Carol Herald was the 'she' in question, because she was the one who made me interested in their hobby."

"And why would you blame her when you were the one who took part in the sessions of your own free will?"

"Because I am weak-willed and always seek to blame other people for my failings I suppose," Barry said and tears welled in his eyes.

"Thank you for the honesty, Barry; it's just a pity it couldn't have started earlier."

"It's not easy to be honest if you enjoy stalking other people, which is why it was so wonderful to meet people who shared my interests and who didn't sneer at me all the time. I regret it now of course, but the die is cast and I have a certain reputation around here which will never be expunged from people's minds."

"Well at the rate things are going there won't be many people left in Goat Parva to remember you. Brenda Jargoy has gone missing now and Reverend Strong has disappeared somewhere too."

"Brenda Jargoy is probably over at Langstroth Hall with Lord Avon."

"Does her husband know?"

"I am sure he does, but I reminded him a few days ago just to make sure he hadn't forgotten."

"You did what?"

"I told him about Brenda and Lord Avon, and how he and Carly Waferr were an item."

"You really gave him both barrels, Barry."

"He was being nasty about my photography and my tripod; he even threatened to stuff the tripod up my behind I seem to remember."

"Did he now – your memory is certainly improving,

Barry; you didn't mention this yesterday at least not to me."

"I thought I did – do you think he might have attacked me, Inspector?"

"He might well have done – I will go and ask him after I have finished with you."

"You haven't finished with me then?"

"No, Barry, I haven't, because I am still not convinced about the comment 'why did she do this' – if you'd been referring to Carol Herald starting the group then you wouldn't have said that – you'd have said something like 'why did she get me involved', 'why did I get involved'. The word 'this' has to refer to the fact you'd been smacked on the head."

"But I don't know who hit me – I don't remember seeing anyone else in the woods."

"No smell of perfume or a lightly breaking branch?"

"Nothing – I heard nothing and I don't remember smelling anything either."

"I wonder though if subconsciously you think it was a woman who attacked you."

"You mean that I have been expecting to be attacked by a woman and now that I have been attacked you think my subconscious believes that a woman was involved?"

"Something like that, Barry, but why would a woman attack you?"

"Women have threatened me, Inspector, as I told you yesterday, so perhaps I thought their threat was more real than any of the men's threats."

"Barry, I would like a psychologist to assess you and then perhaps get a hypnotist to talk to you and see what they can find out."

"Well, as long as I don't have to pay for it then I am happy to indulge you, Inspector."

"I will get that organised, Barry." Knowles pulled away the curtains and headed to reception. He asked whether the police psychologist could come and see Barry and was told yes as long as it was in visiting hours. Knowles would organise the hypnotist himself later.

==============

Barnes hadn't had much joy with Tom Jargoy. He'd steadfastly refused to answer questions about Brenda and Barry Janus and where he'd been the previous morning. As regards Carly Waferr he had admitted that she was a friend of his, but nothing more than that. Barnes tried again.

"So, Tom, you maintain that you know nothing about the attack on Barry Janus?"

"I don't know anything about it, Sergeant Barnes, who would want to attack Barry?"

"And you know nothing about giving Carly Waferr Rohypnol yesterday morning?"

"I was nowhere near her, Sergeant Barnes. I did see her, but I wasn't within 50 yards of her."

"She has said something quite different to us, Tom."

"Well she's lying then."

"Why would she lie, Tom? She's a friend of yours after all."

"I don't know why she would lie to you, Sergeant I can't imagine why she would."

"You're both lying, Tom – you're both liars because you're both hiding something from me and from each other."

"I am not lying to anyone."

"You know that Carly Waferr went back to the woods yesterday after she left you; she went back to find the mobile phone she left there when you were having your way with her; she couldn't find the phone and headed towards the animal shelter to tell your daughter, Wendy, that the phone she stole had been stolen. Carly was asked by Wendy to steal the phone so that the owner of the phone, Adelaide Hills, couldn't report to the police Wendy and her friends' raid on the animal research farm on the river."

"What are you asking me?"

"Whether any of what I said is news to you or whether you were aware of it all?"

"It's all conjecture, Sergeant, you're saying something

138

happened and presenting it as fact – I don't know whether what you're saying is true or not, do I?"

"You having your way with Carly Waferr yesterday morning is not conjecture; it's a fact."

"I deny that ever happened."

"Do you deny running along Sharrock Lane yesterday morning around 9am and looking anxious as you headed into your home?" Knowles had come into the room without the other two being completely aware of what was happening.

Tom Jargoy was very calm.

"You asking me or your Sergeant here?"

"You, Tom, Barnes was with me so he has an alibi. You on the other hand have nothing, nothing at all, other than a police constable who will say in court, under oath, that the defendant was seen running along Sharrock Lane at the aforementioned time with the aforementioned anxious look on his aforementioned visage. That's a fact; that will happen, you had better believe it. You were seen."

"Since when has it been a crime to look anxious in public or to run in public?"

"Since you had just smacked Barry Janus on the head five minutes before," replied Knowles.

"You can't prove anything – you will have to let me go or charge me."

"We will charge you once we have your fingerprints lifted from his bag that you threw into the tree stump."

"Circumstantial evidence."

"And the circumstances were you smacking Barry Janus on the head with a blunt instrument."

"You can't prove anything; time to put up or shut up. What will it be?"

"Well, Tom, I thank you for outlining the options available to me at this time – I select 'shut up' – officer please take Mr Jargoy here to the cells and shut him up in them until such time as he wants to see his lawyer or he believes he can tell us more about the attempted murder of Barry Janus."

"I thought he was dead – you said he was dead." Tom Jargoy sounded a little surprised.

"No, we didn't say that, Tom, does that make a difference to you?" Knowles glared at Jargoy looking for a sign of weakness.

"It doesn't make a difference to me," said Tom Jargoy, but he did look slightly anxious for the first time as he was led away by the officer.

"He thought Janus was dead – he thought he was dead; what does that tell us, sir?"

"He did it alright; he thought he was a murderer and now he knows he's not so let's see what our Tom can come up with in the next few hours."

"Has anyone found Brenda Jargoy yet?"

"The house to house search turned up nothing, not even at Langstroth Hall, so she's done a runner by the looks of it, but without any of her belongings, which is odd."

"Where's she gone? Sister? Brother? Parents?"

"Those are all being investigated, Sergeant; I am pretty sure she's done this before, but I can't remember where she went."

"A local pub probably, close, but not too close."

"And we have asked the local diocese where the Rev Strong is and, apparently, he saw the bishop yesterday and will be back today, so I think we should pay our respects as he will be doing afternoon service at St Timothy's soon."

"Sounds a serious business, seeing the Bishop, sounds like a punishment from the Middle Ages - must have been a moral dilemma he couldn't resolve on his own."

"One that needed a higher authority."

"Does he have to tell us what was discussed? Can we charge him, sir?"

"Of course we could, but it's a question of making the charge stick – what would you suggest we charge him with?"

"Withholding information that would help a police investigation into three murders."

"He has to know that the information would help us and his defence would be 'Oh I didn't know that it would help, I am just a man of the cloth' – even if the cloth is in need of a wash because it's stained with blood."

"The jury would be on his side wouldn't they?"

"Yes, Sergeant, they would be, unless we could show that he'd knowingly misled the police in the performance of their duties."

"We should find out what he has to say for himself."

"We will do. Let's have a late lunch and see him after his 2pm service. I always find these discussions easier to stomach after I have eaten. For some reason I fancy a chicken salad."

===========

Reverend Strong had a congregation of 29 for his service, more than the entire population of Goat Parva. In fact, from the village, only Adelaide Hills, minus Bingo, and The Avons were in the church.

As the people filed out they all shook the reverend's hand and thanked him, some with more enthusiasm than others, for his sermon on the love of money being the root of all evil. Knowles and Barnes watched from Knowles' Land Rover. Mrs Hills saw them and came over for a chat.

"Inspector Knowles and Sergeant Barnes, how nice to see you! Bingo and I had a lovely walk this morning along Sharrock Lane to the river and back again. Twice. That's all that's available to us, because you still have everywhere else cordoned off from the murders and the attack on Barry Janus. When will this change, Inspector?"

"Well, the Clem Shapiro site will be opened tomorrow as will the PC Davis site, so that will be two places to walk – the others will be opened later in the week, perhaps on Wednesday."

"Thank you, Inspector, that's much appreciated from both of us."

"Glad to be of service, Mrs Hills…Adelaide," said Knowles with his eyes fixed on Reverend Strong.

"Reverend Strong gave a very good sermon today, Inspector; he seemed rejuvenated somehow, as though a huge weight had been lifted from his shoulders. He's been burdened by lots of problems recently and now he seems as light as air."

"Like an untethered balloon," said Barnes, "he's got rid of the sandbags and anchors and is heading heavenwards again."

"I am not sure about that, Sergeant, but he is happier within himself, a lot happier. Anyway, I should let you get on with your observations."

With that Adelaide Hills crossed over the road and headed the hundred yards to her own front door. Seeing the last worshipper leave the church Knowles and Barnes got out of their vehicle and headed into St Timothy's churchyard where Rev Strong was still standing with his eyes closed by the door savouring the feeling.

"Let's leave him be – he might be in communion with a higher authority at the moment," said Knowles and withdrew behind a yew hedge keeping the Rev Strong in sight through a convenient gap in the branches. He had already learned some observational skills using vegetation from WPC Smythe. Within two minutes the reverend had finished and disappeared inside the church.

Knowles and Barnes found him with his head bowed kneeling at the altar. He was very still. They sat down in a pew and waited although after a minute Knowles suddenly developed a tickly cough, which caught the attention of the reverend.

"Inspector Knowles and Sergeant Barnes – I was expecting you."

"Really? Why were you expecting us, Reverend?"

"Because I have been away for a couple of days, visiting the Bishop, and I understand when I was away a man was found battered and bruised in my churchyard."

"Barry Janus was found in your churchyard, but that's not why we are here. I would like to know what Carol Herald told you about that caused you so much distress and grief and also caused you to lie to my sergeant here when he visited her house and found you digging in her garden?"

"I did lie that day, Inspector, as Carol did come around the corner when Sergeant Barnes was there, but she left immediately."

"But by doing that you almost certainly caused her to die

unnecessarily, Reverend Strong," said Barnes, hoping that he might make the holy man feel a fit of guilt.

"What I did was wrong, Sergeant, and I have asked God for forgiveness."

"And what was the reply?"

"He has suggested that I should not lie again."

"He's like an Agony Uncle sometimes, isn't he Reverend, always there with some helpful advice for those seeking answers?"

"He's there for all of us, Sergeant."

"Well that's good to know," said Knowles, "but as regards more earthly matters, what did Carol Herald tell you that caused you such consternation?"

Reverend Strong raised his eyebrows slightly and then nodded his head, almost as though he was giving himself permission to tell the police what he knew.

"One week ago, Carol came to me in a highly agitated state; she was involved in a plot to raid the animal research centre down at the farm by the river – she didn't want to break the law, but wanted to help those poor animals in their distressed state. What bothered her more than this though was that two of the other girls at the animal shelter were rather fanatical about the whole raid, but were excluding the other girl from all knowledge of the raid."

"Which two girls were involved in the planning of the raid?"

"She said that Yasmin and Wendy were involved and that they wanted to keep Andrea in the dark, because they felt she would tell the police and that she wasn't trustworthy enough. Carol thought they were being divisive and should tell Andrea, but the other two wouldn't hear of it – words were spoken and Carol felt threatened by those other two."

"You're quite sure that it was Yasmin and Wendy who were involved and that Andrea wasn't involved?"

"100% sure, Inspector, I was surprised too especially regarding Wendy who's so conflicted about her parentage."

"Indeed she is, Reverend Strong, but that doesn't give her the right to break the law, as though that would somehow make up for her lack of definitive parentage."

"Why don't they run a DNA test," asked Barnes, "wouldn't that prove conclusively who the father was?"

"That would require a deal of co-operation and that's not been forthcoming as yet," replied Knowles.

Barnes' phone rang – he went outside to take the call.

"I have told you all I know, Inspector; Carol did swear me to secrecy of course, but as she's now with her maker I don't feel too guilty about telling you."

"I am glad you did Reverend – this is highly useful information that has helped significantly with the investigation of the murders."

Barnes came back in smiling broadly. "We should go to the station; Tom Jargoy would like to talk to us."

"Would he now," said Knowles, "well I think it only polite that we go and listen to what he has to say."

Knowles and Barnes thanked the reverend and left the church. Behind them Reverend Strong smiled and shed a tear, before saying a prayer to his god. A massive weight had been lifted from his shoulders – he would sleep easier.

===========

In the vehicle on the way back to Scoresby, Knowles and Barnes discussed what they had just been told by Reverend Strong.

"So, Inspector, what do you reckon about what we've just been told?"

"Well, Barnesy, I think we might know why Carol Herald was bumped off; either the two girls did it to silence her or Andrea did it as revenge because Carol didn't tell her about the raid, possibly coupled with the belief that Carol was cruel to animals."

"How would Yasmin and Wendy have found out about Carol telling Reverend Strong? He wouldn't have told anyone; his conscience wouldn't have allowed it – he had a hard enough time telling us didn't he?"

"My guess would be they followed her and heard her telling him – they probably didn't trust her completely and followed her."

"Stalking a stalker – this gets just plain weirder. And how would Andrea have found out about the planned raid, if everyone was supposed to keep stumm about it?"

"Oh, god – she would have to have followed Carol too. Can you imagine that?"

"But surely it's either Wendy and Yasmin or Andrea who overheard, not both?"

"Yes, I hope so, whoever overheard Carol talking to Rev Strong almost certainly killed her."

"And what about the first two, Clem and PC Davis? Were they just practice or a cover up, like the ABC Murders?"

"That's Agatha Christie isn't it? Where have I seen that book recently?"

"At Adelaide Hills' house; she had a few murder/mysteries on her bookcase including that one."

"Good spotting, Barnesy, are you sure? You're not just saying that?"

"Absolutely sure."

"Right, at the station ask WPC Smythe to get around to Bingo's owner's house and take those books as evidence; there might be some interesting fingerprints on them."

"Plastic bag job it is, sir."

"Good – of course it could just be a red herring – whoever of those three is the murderer could just have snapped and decided to kill the local people who mistreat their animals. That might be the reason and the raid isn't even a consideration."

"What do we do, pull in the girls altogether or one at a time?"

"We take Andrea and Yasmin first and Wendy Jargoy afterwards, once the other two have been released. Wendy is more easily influenced by other people; I doubt she's involved in killing anyone, but the other two are more controlling. Once we've finished with Tom Jargoy we go and grab those two."

"Sounds like a plan, sir."

"Here we are – which room is Tom Jargoy in?"

"Room 3 – still taking the stairs, sir?"

"Yes, I will see you down there – stop by at WPC Smythe's desk and ask her to go to Goat Parva, would you?"

===========

In interview room 3 Tom Jargoy sat with his elbows on the table leaning his chin on his clasped hands. His lawyer sat impassively waiting for the interview to begin. Knowles arrived first and switched on the tape machine, stating the date and time that the interview began. Barnes soon arrived and gave Knowles a 'thumbs-up' regarding sending Smythe to see Adelaide Hills.

"So, Tom Jargoy, Sergeant Barnes and I would like to hear what you have to say regarding the attack on Barry Janus."

Jargoy looked at his lawyer who raised his eyebrows.

"Yesterday morning I was going past Barry Janus' house in my van, when I saw him running out of his house through the back door into the woods, so I pulled over and followed him – your guy was round the front so didn't see me. Barry isn't the most athletic person in the world, so I soon caught him up. I was still angry with him because of some comments he made to me last week about my wife and Lord Avon. I hit him with a thick branch, threw his bag in the tree stump, and chucked the branch into the river. He wasn't moving – I thought about going back to my van through the woods but thought your guy would be heading my way, so I ran along Sharrock Lane to home and then went through the back door into the woods, around Mrs Hills' house, and back to my van before the rest of your troops arrived. I drove off towards Scoresby, but turned at the next right as I didn't want your lot seeing me driving out of Goat Parva."

"Spur of the moment decision, Tom?"

"Yes, it was – I couldn't believe my luck when I saw him."

"I'll bet you couldn't – the anger hadn't dissipated over the previous days, Tom?"

"No, not at all – he was going to pay for sneering at me."

"Has anyone else sneered at you recently? Clem Shapiro,

146

Carol Herald, or PC Davis for example – did you hit them too, Tom?"

"They did not sneer at me; I did not hit them, only Barry Janus riled me."

"We only have your word for that, Tom, and you told us earlier today that you hadn't seen Barry Janus let alone hit him, so bearing in mind your previous utterances today, I am afraid that I don't believe you when you say that you haven't hit anyone else. The only reason that you have confessed now is because you know that Barry is not dead, whereas earlier today you thought you were being accused of murder."

The lawyer spoke to Tom Jargoy in a soft whisper and then addressed the two officers.

"My client has admitted attacking this Barry Janus character and denies attacking anyone else; I must insist that he be charged with the attack he admits to and that you find evidence to support your other assertions before speaking to him again on that subject."

Knowles nodded and stated the time the interview ended before switching off the tape machine.

"Sergeant Barnes please formally charge Tom Jargoy with a pre-meditated attack on Barry Janus; take him upstairs to the duty sergeant."

Knowles left the room and walked up the stairs to his office. He sat down and looked at a report on his desk. Suddenly a thought hit him. *I am not breathing heavily after walking up the stairs*. He stared at the report for a few seconds without focusing on any of the words; his new regime was working. He was awoken from his reverie by his phone ringing; it was WPC Smythe.

"'Allo, WPC Smythe, I was just having a quiet moment then – my diet and exercise regime is working; I am not out of breath after walking up the stairs."

"Congratulations, sir, that's a good start, of course even the longest journey begins with a small step."

"Thank you for deflating me, Constable, now how can I possibly help you?"

"Well, I am at Adelaide Hills' house – she wasn't too

thrilled to see me; anyway, I have taken the books you asked for, including the ABC Murders by Agatha Christie, and then she told me that she'd found something in Bingo's kennel…"

"…What has that bastard dog found now…hold on could it have been planted there by Carly Waferr? Anyway, sorry I interrupted, what was it that was found in the delightful Bingo's kennel?"

"It was a glove, sir, a right-handed glove."

"A…right-handed…glove. Does it have teeth marks on it?"

"There are teeth marks on the glove."

"And do they fit Bingo the dog's teeth pattern?"

"I will try and find out, sir, I will just put the phone down for a moment."

Knowles heard some growling, a couple of shouts of "Bingo let go", and then there was an ominous silence.

"Hello, sir, Bingo is very attached to the glove and the teeth marks on the glove do seem to be his. Mrs Hills is trying to get the glove from him now…oh she's just managed it. Thank you, Mrs Hills."

"Remind me again, WPC Smythe, where did Adelaide Hills get Bingo from and when?"

Knowles heard Smythe ask the questions, but didn't quite hear the answers.

"Mrs Hills, Adelaide, sorry, she obtained Bingo from the animal shelter in Madeley Waterless about two years ago."

"And how old is the glove would you say?"

"It's well used, sir, nowhere near new."

"Right, well please put the glove in a plastic bag and bring it back with yourself and the books."

"Will do, sir. Is there anything else for me to do?"

"Yes, tomorrow morning, Monday morning, meet me and Barnesy at the Madeley Waterless Animal Shelter at 9am. Bring the glove with you. Leave the books with Forensics and ask for them to find some fingerprints."

"Will do, sir, see you then."

"You will do."

Knowles rang off and waited for Barnes to return from charging Tom Jargoy. Once that happened, he went over what would take place the following day. They'd meet Smythe at the animal shelter take Andrea and Yasmin into custody for questioning separately and then let them go, unless something strange happened and they confessed. Then Wendy Jargoy would be questioned afterwards, on her own, but she would not be allowed to see or meet the other two. Hopefully, they would learn something significant from these interviews and be able to charge someone with three murders.

Chapter 10

Monday, 9am

Knowles, Barnes, and WPC Smythe arrived at the animal shelter at Madeley Waterless in three separate vehicles. They parked in a line and sauntered nonchalantly to the reception where Andrea was checking the till.

"Hello, Andrea, are you on your own today?" asked Barnes.

"Yasmin is in the stables…"

"…With Edgar?"

"Yes, that's correct, Sergeant, and Wendy is checking the kennels."

"Andrea, I would like you to accompany the WPC here to our Scoresby station – we have a number of questions we would like to ask you in connection with the three murders that have recently taken place at Goat Parva. We are not arresting you or charging you with any specific crime, but you will be helping us with our enquiries."

"Am I being arrested or is it up to me whether I go?"

"It's entirely voluntary at this stage, so you can refuse."

"But if I refuse, will you then arrest me, in which case I have to go?"

Barnes looked at Knowles, who smiled.

"Andrea, who knows what the future holds for us? We just want a friendly chat with you, Andrea – you can tell us things, we can tell you things. When you're at the police station voluntarily you're entitled to send a message to your family or a friend telling them where you are and to receive free legal advice from a solicitor. If you go to the police station voluntarily, you can leave at any time."

"Unless you arrest me!"

"What have you done to cause us to do that, Andrea?"

"OK, I will come with you, I don't have anything to hide, but I am wondering what you will be telling me."

"You will be surprised I think. Please follow the WPC – we will tell Wendy and Yasmin."

WPC Smythe accompanied Andrea to the police car. They drove out of the entrance and headed back to Scoresby.

Barnes was heading towards the stables, but Knowles stopped him short.

"Where do you think you're going, Sergeant?"

"To see Yasmin, sir."

"No you're not, put your tongue away, go and tell Wendy she's going to be on her own for a while, and then go back to the station and chat with Andrea; let her know about the possible raid on the research farm and see how she reacts."

"Right, understood, sir." Barnes turned on his heel and headed to the kennels.

Knowles walked into the stables and saw Yasmin scrubbing the horse she'd been washing the previous time they'd visited.

"Inspector Knowles, how can I help you this time?"

"Well, Yasmin, this time is slightly different to last time. I would like you to accompany me to our Scoresby station – we have a number of questions we would like to ask you in connection with the three murders that have recently taken place at Goat Parva. We are not arresting you or charging you with any specific crime, but you will be helping us with our enquiries."

"Am I being arrested or is it up to me whether I go?"

"It's entirely voluntary at this stage - you can refuse."

"But if I refuse, will you then arrest me, in which case I have to go?"

Knowles smiled – someone had been providing lessons.

"Yasmin, we want a friendly chat with you – you can tell us things, we can tell you things. When you're at the police station voluntarily, you're entitled to send a message to your family or a friend telling them where you are and to receive free legal advice from a solicitor. If you go to the police station voluntarily, you can leave at any time."

"OK, I will come with you, I don't have anything to hide – what will you be telling me?"

Knowles shrugged. "I am sure there will be something of interest."

"I should tell the other two I am leaving for a while."

"They know already; hop into my vehicle and we will be there in ten minutes."

As they drove away, Wendy Jargoy came out from the kennels and stared after them – she looked very afraid.

=============

Barnes decided to chat with Andrea in interview room number 1, but without switching on the tape machine. He did press the 'Record' button on his phone and placed that inside his jacket pocket.

"Andrea – thank you for coming voluntarily to the station today; I do have some questions regarding your possible involvement in the three murders in Goat Parva over the past week."

"I have not been involved in any murders, Sergeant, what motivation would I have for killing three people?"

"They hurt animals, you were upset with them and so you killed them."

"No – I couldn't do that."

"Were you aware that Yasmin, Wendy, and Carol were planning a raid on the research farm downstream of Goat Parva in the next few days?"

"What!!! Where were they planning on putting the rescued animals? Not in our shelter I hope. You are not serious, Sergeant Barnes, you are joking?"

"I believe not, so I would suggest to you that you found out about this raid, were upset that Carol had organised this escapade without you, and decided to finish her off, but that you needed to cover this fact up, so you killed two other stalkers as a disguise."

"I didn't know this was being planned, I had no idea, I didn't know – the three of them kept me in the dark, how could my colleagues do that?"

"You're telling me you had no idea there was going to be a raid, which was why you asked Carly Waferr to steal

Adelaide Hills' phone? You were watching myself and WPC Smythe in Culpepper's Woods two days ago and you saw Carly Waferr was unable to find the phone when she lost it? You told her not to go to the animal shelter."

"I was in Culpepper's Woods two days ago – I admit I saw Carly and that she was searching for something, but I'd no idea what it was she was looking for. I saw she was upset and she looked lost, so I suggested she go home through the woods. I didn't know there was going to be a raid and I have no idea what you mean about stealing a phone from Adelaide Hills. I am bewildered."

"Why have you been so hostile towards our investigation?"

"I've had a few run-ins with the police over the years, largely because of cannabis."

"Wait a minute please, Andrea."

Barnes picked up his phone and called WPC Smythe, asking her to bring the glove into the interview room. He also asked her to go to the animal shelter and come back with Wendy Jargoy, believing that his interview with Andrea was almost over.

WPC Smythe came in with the glove and placed it on the table. Andrea recognised the glove straightaway.

"Where did you find this, we lost this almost a week ago?"

"Whose is it?"

"It's the shelter's really, but Yasmin and Wendy use it more often than I do."

"We found it in the kennel of Bingo the retriever, Mrs Hills' dog, who found the three bodies."

Andrea threw the glove away from her as though it was poisoned.

"You mean it was used to kill someone and somehow dropped and then Bingo found the glove and took it home."

"Yes, he probably hunted it out because he recognised the smell of the shelter; Mrs Hills bought Bingo from the shelter where you work."

"That's correct. Oh my goodness, who have I been

working with these past few years? They've killed three people including one of their own colleagues. I am scared now; I can't go back – are you going to arrest the others, I mean Wendy and Yasmin?"

"We don't have any evidence, Andrea. The glove is useful, but as you all used it then we can't prove anything beyond reasonable doubt. Unless you know something?"

"I don't know anything that would help you; they have kept me in the dark about this raid, so they are evidently very good at what they do. Why did they kill Carol?"

"I am not sure they did, but to answer your question I think she must have told someone else about the plans."

"Please take me home, I feel nauseated, the others will have to look after the place, but I will have to face them at some point, until they're arrested – when will you do that?"

"We need evidence, Andrea, and I think you should go back to work; we have a plainclothes person there posing as a customer, so that's of some reassurance I hope. It would look odd if you went home after talking to the police."

"It would I suppose – will you take me back now?"

"Yes, I will do, let's go out of the station the back way and take an alternative route back to Madeley."

Andrea nodded her full agreement. Barnes dropped off the glove at WPC Smythe's desk and texted this information to Knowles. They then walked out of the station, just as Knowles started his chat with Yasmin next door, in interview room 2.

============

"Yasmin, please note that you are here voluntarily and can leave at any time during our chat."

"I understand, Inspector."

"Right, that's good – so when were you planning to raid the animal research farm upstream of Goat Parva?"

"That's an interesting start –well we have talked about it for a long time and I thought it would definitely take place last Thursday or Friday morning, but there was a murder on Tuesday night/Wednesday morning and we decided to wait

154

because everyone's awareness had been heightened and we were worried that we'd be caught."

"Is that why you asked Carly Waferr to steal Adelaide Hills' phone and blame it on Bingo the dog?"

"Carol asked Carly and she was only too pleased to help, although I wasn't aware that Carly was going to blame the disappearance on poor Bingo."

"We'll have less of the poor Bingo talk, OK?" joked Knowles. "Who was going on the raid with you and Wendy?"

"Carol was meant to be, but I am not sure she would have gone with us."

"She was dead on Friday morning, Yasmin."

"I know, Inspector Knowles."

"Did Carol tell anyone about the raid, Yasmin?"

"Well I haven't told anyone, Wendy hasn't, so if you know then Carol must have told someone else, who has told you."

"Does Carol talking like that make you angry, Yasmin?"

"It's unfortunate, especially as we could have got into trouble because she talked to the wrong person."

"Why did you exclude Andrea from your plans?"

"She would have been against it from the very beginning; she might have told the police, but when all is said and done all she is interested in is making sure our animals are OK. She was and is uninterested in the plight of animals in general."

"Who did Carol tell, do you think?"

"Probably her stalking friends like Clem Shapiro, PC Davis, and Barry Janus."

"A motive for murder perhaps, Yasmin?"

"Who can tell, Inspector?"

"Excuse me," said Knowles, "I just have to make a phone call." He called the duty sergeant who arranged for the glove, still in a plastic bag, to be brought to Knowles.

"Yasmin, do you recognise this?"

"Yes, it's the glove that we lost last week. Where was it found?"

"In Bingo the dog's kennel."

"How did it end up there?"

"Bingo the dog took it from one of the murder scenes we think."

Yasmin placed the glove carefully on the desk and stared into the distance.

"Does that mean Carol killed Clem Shapiro and PC Davis?"

"How do you know that Bingo didn't take it from the scene of Carol's murder?"

"I don't, but I am sure we missed the glove on Thursday, Inspector."

"I see – that's good information to have and narrows down the field somewhat."

Knowles glanced down at his phone and saw a text message from WPC Smythe indicating she was bringing Wendy Jargoy into interview room 1. He replied to her to knock on his door, which she did 10 seconds later.

"Yasmin, this is WPC Smythe, she will be driving you back to your place of work – I'd go the back way, Constable, it's quicker. Thank you for the information."

Smythe nodded and Yasmin smiled. Knowles opened the interview room's front door and then peered into room 1 where Wendy Jargoy was looking very tense. This would be an interesting interview.

============

"'Allo, Wendy, how are you feeling this fine day?"

"A little nervous about what you will force me to say."

"I won't force you to say anything, Wendy, you are here voluntarily remember?"

"Where are Yasmin and Andrea?"

"They're not here, Wendy," said Knowles truthfully, "why should that worry you?"

"I feel vulnerable here on my own."

"There's no need, Wendy, now can you tell me about the raid on the animal research farm you were planning with Andrea and Carol?"

"What raid would that be, Inspector?"

"The raid I discussed with Yasmin recently – the one you were going to be part of Wendy Jargoy."

"Oh, that one."

"Yeah that one, Wendy, that raid."

"What do you want to know?"

"Who asked Carly Waferr to steal Mrs Hills' phone?"

"Well that would have been Carol – Mrs Hills would have reported us if she'd had her mobile phone and we'd have disappeared by the time the police arrived by the river if she had to go home to phone you, Inspector."

Knowles smiled.

"Why did you keep Andrea in the dark?"

"Andrea would have told you, Inspector; she isn't active enough for our liking, she tolerates animal research rather than campaigning against it."

"And Carol – was she happy about being part of your half-baked idea to rescue the doggies from the research farm?"

"She was involved; she probably told someone though and we decided to wait and then she was killed on Friday morning and we were short one person, so it was postponed."

"Did you like Carol, Wendy, or did you despise her enough to kill her?"

"I didn't kill her – I couldn't harm another living creature, another sentient being; no that would have been anathema to me."

"But she blabbed about your raid; didn't that make you angry, Wendy?"

"No, Inspector, what I didn't like about Carol was the way she sneered at other people, and shouted at them if they hurt their animals, yet she still associated with those hideous stalkers. Look at Clem Shapiro and how he slaughtered those pigs and that PC Davis who took his dog for a walk in the woods and beat it seven times with a branch."

"Seven times, so seven acorns in the mouth?"

Wendy looked askance at Knowles.

"What do you mean - seven acorns in the mouth?"

"That's what was stuffed in PC Davis' mouth when he was killed, Wendy."

157

"How awful." She shuddered with revulsion.

"Who would have done that?"

"It's the sort of thing that Carol might have done – she was quite vindictive; a week or so ago Poppy came to see me and she was very upset because she had dyed her dog green and then the gardener had mowed it on the lawn and killed it. Poppy was distraught and Carol just laughed at her, asking what she expected if she coloured her dog green and then let it lie on the grass. Yasmin and I couldn't believe how heartless Carol was, especially as Pops was so tearful."

"What did Andrea feel about Carol's behaviour?"

"We didn't tell her, Inspector."

"She wasn't there when Poppy was upset?"

"No, it was her day off I think."

Knowles produced the glove from his jacket pocket and placed it on the table.

Wendy recognised it straightaway.

"Where did you get this from, Inspector?"

"Bingo the dog took it from one of the murder scenes, we think."

"One of the murder scenes; which one?"

"When did you first notice it was missing, Wendy?"

"Thursday morning, I think, as I was brushing the courtyard and needed both gloves as the broom handle has splinters."

"And it was definitely there on Wednesday?"

"Well that's a good question because I didn't use the gloves on Wednesday for anything – at least anything that I can remember, so I can't be definite about the glove being there on Wednesday."

"Thank you, Wendy, I am not sure which murder the glove was used in as Bingo the dog found all three bodies, as I am sure you know."

"Yes, the retriever instinct was working overtime."

"What do you think his instinct was sensing; the smell or smells of a place where he grew up as a puppy perhaps, before going to live with Mrs Hills?"

"I wouldn't know, Inspector, I would have thought he was

just an inquisitive dog who found things when he went for a walk."

"Yes, but it's the reason why he found the bodies that intrigues me – he was finding a familiar smell, the smell of the animal shelter associated with the scene of each of three murders."

"Are you saying that one of us killed those three people?"

"If by 'one of us' you mean yourself, Yasmin, Andrea, and Carol then yes, I am."

"But you can't include Carol can you?"

"Why not, Wendy, why not?"

"Well she didn't kill herself...?"

"No, but she could have committed the first two murders and then been killed herself by another one of you."

"So, there might have been two murderers working at the animal shelter?"

"Yes, it is possible."

"Or three, because three of us could have done one murder each."

"So, which one will you claim then?"

"I am not the murdering kind; just thinking about it gives me goose pimples."

"Which of the others is a murdering kind, would you say?"

"I wouldn't like to say, Inspector; I wouldn't want to build your hopes up too much."

"Thank you for your consideration."

At that moment Knowles' phone rang; it was Barnes calling to ask how things were progressing.

"Wendy – I will just step out of the room a minute, OK?"

Wendy nodded.

"'Allo, Barnesy...how's it going with Wendy? Well I think I have made a point with her, in that Bingo the dog found those bodies because he was following a scent he associated with his lovely days as a puppy at the animal shelter....yes....I know, I appreciate that Carol Herald was murdered and that she was around the other two bodies before Bingo found them and so the scent could have come from her - but Wendy doesn't know that does she? We have not told her. None of them know. Anyway, I will let her go back to the shelter and see what transpires…. I will drive her back. Have two plain clothes officers arrive on the scene just after I leave the shelter – they know my vehicle. I think something might happen now. Anyway, I should go back in there now and finish the interview. I will see you back at the station."

Knowles went back into the interview room where Wendy was leaning on the table with her elbows and with her hands cradling her chin.

"Wendy, I will take you back to the animal shelter, I think I've finished with my questions for the day."

"Inspector, do you really think that one of us at the animal shelter is a murderer?"

"It's highly likely, Wendy, highly likely; it might be you of course."

"It's not me, Inspector, it's not me – but I think I might know who it is; I will have to ponder this." And with that, Wendy Jargoy kept her peace all the way back to the shelter.

============

As Knowles drove out of the shelter gates, he saw the plain clothes vehicle parked about 50 yards away. He pulled over to speak with them.

"'Allo there, the three women in the animal shelter are all possible suspects in three murders, and I think that we may have just ruffled a few feathers, so please keep a close eye on events particularly if two of them try and corner the third one. Understood? Good – do phone me if something happens and we'll be over in a jiffy."

When Knowles returned to his desk he saw that Barnes was on the phone, so he decided to write his version of what Wendy Jargoy had said in her interview. When Barnes put the receiver down he looked rather bemused.

"So, Brenda Jargoy is back in Goat Parva and is serving in the shop. I just received a phone call from Adelaide Hills to this effect."

"Don't tell me - Bingo found she was at home?"

"As a matter of fact, that's exactly what happened. Bingo barked at the door of the shop until Mrs Jargoy opened it and let him in."

"Why would he do that? Where did he go when he went inside?"

"Mrs Hills didn't say, sir."

"Right, well we should find out, Sergeant. I wonder whether we shouldn't take Bingo to the animal shelter and see how he behaves towards the three women. After all, I think the reason he found the bodies was because of a familiar smell from his days as a puppy."

"Sounds like a plan, sir."

"Right, let's go to Goat Parva, grab Bingo and Mrs Hills, find out why the dog was so keen to find Mrs Jargoy, and then head to the animal shelter."

"Shouldn't we find out where Brenda Jargoy has been, sir?"

"Yes, that too. I think she went to her sister's place in Northampton for a couple of days myself but you can ask her nicely, Sergeant."

"Wasn't that one of the places that Tom Jargoy mentioned regarding animal shelters that Wendy had been in contact with?"

"Indeed it was, Barnesy – all beginning with 'N' - but what's the connection between Brenda and animal shelters?"

"We shall have to find that out too."

===========

Knowles and Barnes drove to Goat Parva and parked outside the village shop; they went inside and saw Brenda Jargoy serving a female customer and waited until she departed before approaching.

"'Allo, Brenda, how are you?"

"I'm fine thank you, Inspector, and how are you?"

"Fair to middling as usual, Brenda, fair to middling – I understand you have just been away for a while – where did you go?"

"I went to Northampton to see my sister."

"Without an overnight bag or change of clothes?"

"I'm a regular visitor, so I have a number of clothes over there already."

"Why would Bingo the dog be determined to get into your shop do you think?"

"He was just being a retriever, Inspector Knowles."

"If that's all then you won't mind him coming back, will you, Brenda?"

Brenda looked unsure about this.

"Something wrong, Mrs Jargoy," said Barnes, "something you wouldn't want him to retrieve perhaps?"

"I'm not sure what he'd be interested in, so by all means bring him back here and let's find out shall we?"

"Right, well don't go back to Northampton in the next ten minutes, Brenda – we'll just go and fetch him."

Brenda Jargoy smiled wanly as the two officers exited her shop.

"What do you reckon, Barnesy?"

"Brought something back from Northampton, sir, that's what I think."

"Such as what though?"

"Information perhaps about where they would meet the raiding party on the riverbank?"

"But they're surely not going to go ahead, now we know what's going on?"

"Double bluff perhaps? They know we know and they think we think they won't go ahead with the raid for this reason, but they are still planning it."

"Sounds like a complicated situation. What will they do without Mrs Hills' phone in their possession?"

"Go earlier, leave the farm earlier, take fewer animals."

"Right, well let's discuss this after we've been to the shelter in Madeley."

Barnes knocked and heard a scratching of claws on the inside of the door as Bingo tried to burrow through it. Mrs Hills shouted "Stop it, Bingo" and the door opened.

Mrs Hills beamed at the policemen. "Officers, how can I help you, he's not found anything of interest to you today, I am sure?"

"Not yet, Mrs Hills…Adelaide, but in a strange twist to recent events I would really like our beloved Bingo to find something for us, or perhaps someone of interest, while we watch him – could you bring him with you, please, and follow Sergeant Barnes and myself?"

"Where are we going on our little adventure, Inspector?"

"Firstly to the village shop and then to the animal shelter at Madeley."

Mrs Hills disappeared inside and was then almost dragged outside carrying her coat by Bingo who sensed something was afoot and was excited.

They headed to the shop and when Bingo was within ten feet of the door he began to bark and strain even more on his lead.

Barnes opened the door and Bingo thrust inside past the counter into the back, his nose twitching – eventually he stopped and barked at a large laundry basket.

"You wouldn't like to open that would you, Brenda?" said Knowles, looking at Mrs Jargoy with a piercing stare.

She opened it and Bingo started to bark, but with a more contented sound, as though he'd found what his nose had told him was there.

Barnes peered inside and saw two overalls, similar to the ones worn at the shelter. He put on a pair of plastic see-through gloves and gingerly removed the first overall, which hadn't been washed. He checked the pockets and found nothing; Knowles stopped Bingo pawing at the overall.

"Whose is this, Brenda?" asked Knowles.

"It's Wendy's, Inspector, as is the other overall in there; they were here when I came back."

"There's blood on the collar and right sleeve, sir."

"You are a clever dog, Bingo," said Mrs Hills.

"Bag them up, Barnesy, and get them to Forensics when we go back."

Barnes checked the other overall and these pockets were also empty. He placed the overalls in separate bags and took them outside, placing them carefully in the back of Knowles' Land Rover.

"Are you sure they're Wendy's overalls and not Andrea's

or Yasmin's? I got the impression that they shared everything?"

"I meant Wendy brought them home, Inspector Knowles, that's what I meant."

"Right. Do you know where Tom is, Brenda?"

"He's out of the house; I don't really care where he is."

"Well you should; he's at Scoresby station and has been charged with attacking Barry Janus."

"He did that? That doesn't surprise me – what a bastard he is; I'm not visiting him; I am thinking of living closer to my sister and selling this place."

"Go to any animal shelters while you were there in Northampton?" asked Barnes.

"We'll just wait outside," said Mrs Hills and began to drag Bingo out of the room, "Bingo can get us out of here I'm sure."

"I did, Sergeant Barnes; I was asked to give a letter to Wendy."

"We'll take that from you, Brenda, we're going to see her now, and you know something – you could come too. There's plenty of room in the back of my jalopy."

"Sergeant, just accompany Mrs Jargoy to collect her letter and make sure she's not about to phone her daughter."

Barnes shrugged as Brenda Jargoy looked at him. She walked into the next room and returned brandishing a large envelope.

"Here you are, Sergeant, and I am ready to go when you are."

"Right let's go," ordered Knowles. "Brenda, you sit in the front seat and Sergeant, you can sit in the back with Adelaide and Bingo the dog." Knowles then phoned the plain clothes people at the shelter and asked them to ensure none of the employees left especially after Knowles and his party arrived.

When everyone was seated Knowles reversed his Land Rover out into the road and headed off to Madeley Waterless with Bingo the dog enjoying the wind blowing through his fur.

"Is this your own vehicle, Inspector, or is it a police vehicle?" asked Mrs Hills brightly.

"It's mine, but I do have a portable siren I can stick to the side should I need to make people aware of my presence."

"I wouldn't have thought you'd need the siren very much around here, Inspector, there's not that much going on is there?"

"A week ago I would have agreed, Adelaide, but not now – there's something going around here all the time."

"You make it sound like a den of iniquity, Inspector."

"It is, Adelaide, though once we catch the murderer I think things will calm down a little."

"And when will you catch the murderer, Inspector Knowles?" asked Brenda Jargoy.

"Well it will be very soon now, I think, very soon indeed, and I am almost certain who it is."

"Will you share your thoughts, Inspector?"

Knowles shook his head – he wasn't a very good poker player especially when he was bluffing.

Knowles pulled up outside the animal shelter and everyone got out. Knowles reached into his pocket and brought out the glove. He removed it from the plastic bag and dangled it in front of Bingo, who started to bark. This set off some barking inside the shelter.

"Let's see who we can find," said Knowles. "Adelaide, would you like to go ahead of us?"

"Where do I go?"

"Towards the reception for a start I think."

Bingo started to pull Mrs Hills. Wendy Jargoy came out of the door and stopped dead in her tracks when she saw her mother. Bingo pawed at the ground and barked twice, but didn't jump up at Wendy.

"Mother, what are you doing with the police?"

"We're helping her deliver this letter to you from your friends in Northampton, Wendy," said Barnes handing her the envelope. "Still going ahead with the raid then? Taking the animals down to Northampton are we?"

"This will be the time and date we will meet them by the river bank; they'll take the animals with them."

"Why the subterfuge, getting your own mum to be the go-between?"

"We are convinced the phone is being tapped and the conversations recorded, and we don't trust the post, so this was the best way of doing it."

"What about a racing pigeon with a note strapped to its leg?"

"Very funny," said Wendy and patted Bingo on the head.

Andrea came walking across to the group. Bingo barked three times though he stayed where he was.

"Hello everyone, what's the occasion?"

"Just a family visit," said Wendy, "nothing too exciting."

"Hello, Bingo," said Andrea, "how are you – not been back here in a while have you?"

Bingo barked as she patted him on the head.

"What's that you've got there, Wendy?" said Andrea.

"Just something my mum delivered for me," came the reply.

"Which needed a police escort? Must be important, Wendy. Let's have a look."

"It's personal, Andrea, it's personal, please respect that."

"OK, 'nuff said, Wendy – something for Yasmin and you to share I suppose."

"Something like that."

"Where is Yasmin by the way?" asked Knowles.

"She's helping a customer choose a cat at the moment," replied Andrea, "I'm sure she won't be long."

"It's important to choose the right kind of cat," said Barnes knowing that Knowles was bound to say something on the subject, which he lost no time in doing.

"I think it's important to choose a cat full stop as they are wonderful animals – most cats are very similar and need little looking after, except for their meals of course. They don't need taking for a walk and can wash themselves rather than being taken to a spa. They also don't howl uncontrollably for no good reason, unlike certain other animals I can think of."

"A cat wouldn't have found the bodies though would it, Inspector?" said Mrs Hills patting Bingo.

"No, it would have minded its business and a human being would have found them and left them alone, rather than taking evidence away."

166

Barnes thought about interjecting on Bingo's behalf, but decided not to. At that moment Yasmin appeared and Bingo began to bark and strain at his leash. He tried to head towards Yasmin, but Mrs Hills managed to restrain him.

"Why do you think Bingo's so keen to see you, Yasmin?" asked Knowles.

"He remembers me from his time here at the shelter I suppose."

"Really, well he didn't greet Wendy and Andrea the same way," continued Knowles.

Mrs Jargoy gasped and stared at Yasmin.

"I showed Bingo the glove that he found at one of the crime scenes just before we came in here, Yasmin. He sniffed the glove and I would say that he associates that glove with you given his reaction. To my mind, you were the last person to wear that glove, which puts you at the scene of a murder."

"Oh my, it was you, I wondered why you reacted so badly when Carol asked you where the other glove was. You were aware that you'd made a mistake," said Wendy.

"That's why Carol had to go – she'd blabbed about the raid and you thought she would talk about the glove to someone," said Barnes.

"Oh yes, the secretive raid that most people knew about," said Andrea.

"Do you have anything to say, Yasmin?" enquired Knowles.

"Not without a lawyer present," said Yasmin, "not without a lawyer."

A couple came up carrying a rather large ginger cat with green eyes.

"Nice cat," said Knowles, "what's the name?"

"Pebbles," said the man.

"Why is it called Pebbles?" asked Barnes. "Why would you call a ginger cat, Pebbles?"

"It's a nice name for a cat," said Knowles. "Anyway, Constables, that's good cover buying a cat – excellent work - could you take Mrs Jargoy, Mrs Hills, and her hound back to Goat Parva please?"

"Actually, Inspector, I think I would like to walk back via

the newly opened ruined monastery at Manton Rempville –
it's only two miles away and Bingo needs a good, long walk.
It will be a reward for helping you to catch the murderer."

"If Adelaide's not going with the constables, can I go
instead – I'd like to be with my mum and talk about possibly
visiting my father?" asked Wendy.

"Sounds like everything's resolved then. Sergeant Barnes
read Yasmin her rights and ensure she understands that she is
being arrested on suspicion of committing three murders.
Then she can come with us to the station and meet her
lawyer."

Chapter 11

Monday, afternoon

Yasmin sat next to her lawyer in interview room 2 at Scoresby Police Station. She looked calm, but her eyes were quite red. Knowles knocked on the door and went inside followed by Barnes. A constable stood by the wall with his arms crossed. The artificial light flickered.

Knowles switched on the tape machine and said the date, the time and those who were present.

"Yasmin Hutton – you have been charged with the murders of Clem Shapiro at around 11pm on Tuesday, September 22nd – of Roger Davis at around 7am on Thursday, September 24th, and of Carol Herald at around 7:15am on Friday, September 25th. What is your reaction to this charge?"

"My reaction is that I am guilty as charged. I just wish there were more people willing to stick up for all the animals in the world that are being harmed by the human race and its inconsiderate, selfish, and uncaring attitude towards the rest of the living creatures on the surface of the Earth. We are only interested in animals if we can make money from them. Still that's the capitalist way – making money is the overriding concern."

"Why Clem Shapiro?"

"He mistreated his pigs and killed them cruelly without any dignity – he had a cute piglet called Rosemary and we wanted her at the shelter, so we could rear her properly, but he killed her and put the head in the window of his shop with a rose in her mouth. I hit him very hard with a stone and enjoyed seeing the heartless bastard die – I put a flower in his mouth to mimic his murder of Rosemary."

"What did you do with his golf seat?"

"I threw it in the river – he was watching that tart and never heard me behind him. He was preoccupied you could

169

say. I put the stone into the seat and it sank quite effectively."

"How did you know he was going to be there?"

"We were scouting the river bank one night two weeks ago for landing places and Carol told me Shapiro was always there on a Tuesday night...watching."

"And PC Davis?"

"He beat his dog, Bruno, in the woods with tree branches and that dog was so lovely. Davis was a pervert who enjoyed watching Mr Greggs bending over in the woods – he was captivated by it and wasn't aware of me. I stuffed acorns in his mouth and watched the life leak out of the lecher."

"What did you hit him with?"

"Another stone; not very original am I? I buried it in Culpepper's Woods on the way to the shelter."

"Again, how did you know he was going to be there?"

"Carol told me that Davis was a regular viewer of Mr Greggs on Thursdays and Fridays, so I just waited in the woods on that day and saw him and waited for the opportunity to strike. I was almost seen by Poppy, but she was in some kind of trance and so I was able to evade her. When Carol heard that Davis had died I was sure she knew that it was me and so she had to go as well before she told someone, like she had done with the raid. I followed her on the Friday and smacked her on the head too. Another stone for the river."

"Indeed there was – another murder weapon washed clean by the water."

"Sounds almost biblical, Inspector."

"How did you lose the glove, Yasmin?"

"After I hit Shapiro, I noticed that the stone had marked the gloves, and so I cleaned them as I wanted to return them to the shelter in the same state that I found them in, so as not to arouse suspicion. I presume one fell out of my pocket when I was moving the golf seat. Very careless – I even went back the following morning to find it, but there were too many people around like Barry Janus, Carly, Carol, Mrs Hills, and your Sergeant of course, so I couldn't rectify the problem."

"Thank you, Yasmin, for your remarkably open reconstruction of each of the murders. I don't like people who harm animals either but I don't kill them."

Knowles looked at Barnes and nodded – he had heard enough to know she was now being completely honest. He closed the interview.

===========

A few weeks later Sergeant Barnes was in the office early one morning doing some paperwork for a case involving a serial burglar, whom he had caught in Flixton.

The phone rang – it was a number he recognised.

"Hello, how are you…. What?..."

===========

Inspector Knowles was at home reading through some paperwork while having a nice light breakfast of yoghourt, fruit, and toast. His diet was working well and he had lost fifteen pounds already. His mobile phone rang and he let it ring a few times. Eventually though he answered - Gemma had glared at him as the noise had woken her up.

"'Allo, Barnesy, how are things with you? I am sitting down ....a body has been found at the ruins at Manton Rempville…who found the body? …What again, not another one? I don't believe it."

Knowles put the phone down and pushed the paperwork aside. It would have to wait - there was another murder to investigate. He stroked Gemma and thought how lucky he was not to own a dog that needed constant attention.

He walked to the front door shaking his head at how trouble seemed to follow some people, or in this case a dog, around.

Made in the USA
Las Vegas, NV
29 December 2023

83673755R00102